W9-AWZ-094

the
house *on*
apple hill
lane

ELIZABETH
BROMKE

This book is a work of fiction. Names, characters, places, and events are products of the author's imagination. Any resemblance to locations, events, or people (living or dead) is purely coincidental.

Copyright © 2021 Elizabeth Bromke

All rights reserved.

Cover design by Red Leaf Cover Design

The reproduction or distribution of this book without permission is a theft. If you would like to share this book or any part thereof (reviews excepted), please contact us through our website:

elizabethbromke.com

THE HOUSE ON APPLE HILL LANE

Publishing in the Pines

White Mountains, Arizona

For my neighbors.

1973

Tires rubbed on fresh asphalt as the scenery out the window blurred. The little girl in soft braids tucked her pale pink dress tighter around her skinny thighs. Her body lurched forward as the driver straightened out the sled of a town car, easing them down a hill.

She was oddly comforted to see that the house sat along the side of a hill. It made sense, since the address of her destination was Apple Hill Lane. This, she confirmed with a careful stare at the crisscross street sign they passed on the corner. Apple Hill Lane. Heaven forbid the driver get lost, or worse.

But no. No such adventure. They'd arrived where they were meant to. On Apple Hill Lane.

Grandad and Nana's street. And on the left, at 696, their house.

She'd never been.

Most children her age visited their grandparents' house every weekend. Or at least for Christmas.

She had never been once in her life.

Until now.

Despite the hill, however, Apple Hill Lane was still partly misnamed, it would appear. Though, she couldn't be certain.

Peering out the bottom slit of the rear window in that strange town car, well, it didn't give her enough of a view to confirm. Still, as far as she could tell, there were no apple trees lining the street. And though it did start at the top of a hill, most of the houses on the street were at the bottom of that hill.

Only one stood at the top. Only one house on the hill. Grandad and Nana's.

The town car drove down the cul-de-sac and rounded back, parking in front of the house with the numbers 696 running down the side of it.

She scrambled across the seat to the curbside door, stared out the window, and gasped. A full gasp to the point of choking on the smoky air in the hot back seat of the town car with its maroon, velvet fabric.

Never in her life had she seen a house so beautiful. It towered there, at the crest of Apple Hill Lane, stately and royal. She'd seen photographs of palaces in far-off lands, and this house had to be the closest she'd ever come.

1

QUINN, PRESENT DAY

Quinn Whittle smoothed her black tunic down her hips, then set her jaw and narrowed her gaze.

Before her, forty yards away, sat the house. Broad faced and teeming with potential.

She studied it from where she stood at the curb, half a stride from her car. It was the first time she was seeing it. Like *this*, at least.

The shutters stood at odd angles, like crooked teeth in a crowded mouth. One window was boarded in wood that had rotted through long ago. Paint chipped along the eaves and at every corner, every edge.

Quinn swallowed hard and pressed the locking button on her key fob.

Once.

Twice.

Three times.

She stepped onto the narrow strip of grass that separated the street, Apple Hill Lane, from the sidewalk, which separated the world from the private property that was to be her new home.

Glancing right, she noted the other houses on that particular lane in Harbor Hills, Michigan. Each obscured only partially by thick green trees, it was easy to see that 696 was the pit of the neighborhood. White trim and bold colors stood against neatly maintained brick on the house next door. Beyond that, buzzed lawns glowed green in rolling hills all the way down to where the lane curled into a cul-de-sac.

"You must be Quinn!" A woman appeared just down the sidewalk, where Quinn had been looking.

This would be the Realtor. Conveniently, she happened to live one house down. A next-door neighbor. Annette Best with Best on the Block Realty, a company passed down from her father-in-law, it would turn out.

Quinn put on a winning smile and smoothed her tunic a second time, which meant she'd better go ahead and smooth it a third time. For good measure. "Hi." She beamed, her lip catching on her front teeth, forcing her to hold the smile so as not to look like a gummy goof. "I'm so excited," she added after running her tongue around inside of her mouth.

"You *are*?" the woman asked, a trill to her tone, as if

The car lunged forward and back as the driver stepped out, strode around, and popped open her door. Having leaned her whole form against it, she spilled into him. He huffed, helped her straighten, then straightened himself. "Here we are." He gestured his hand up the walk.

Fresh cut grass gave way against the cobblestone clear up to the broad front porch. Like something off of a movie set, the porch held four rocking chairs—all wood and gleaming, polished. One rocked errantly. She was certain, even from that long ways off, that someone had only just pushed out of the chair and left. Was it her grandmother? Nana? Grandfather? Grandad? What would she call them? What would they call her?

Then, it occurred to her, she wasn't entirely sure whether they had ever made one another's acquaintance before. Maybe they had!

She glanced back at the driver, who was removing her single piece of luggage from the trunk of the car. Swallowing, she accepted it, thanked him, and took off toward the front door.

What seemed like an hour later, she arrived at it, and her hand made its way up to the knocker. It froze there, in the air, twitching as if filled with buzzing flies.

The driver's voice carried across the yard. "I'll be off, then."

She wanted to scream back "Wait!" and "What if they don't answer!" and "Don't leave me!"

But it was too late. By the time the words formed on her tongue, the car was rolling up and out of the neighborhood and away from the little girl who was sent to live there, with grandparents she'd maybe never met. On a hill without apples, on Apple Hill Lane.

she was entirely surprised to hear Quinn was *excited* about 696 Apple Hill Lane.

Nodding enthusiastically, Quinn gestured up to the house. "I know. It's—a fixer-upper."

"Oh, I'm going to like you." The woman joined Quinn on a clean square of cement just beyond the squat picket fence that was once probably bright white, like Quinn's features. "I'm Annette Best with Best on the Block. And I tend to prefer fixer-uppers myself." She thrust a hand at Quinn, and Quinn paused just a beat before accepting it.

Annette Best was clean-looking, above all else. A short mousy bob with lots of swish gave her a likable way, and minimal, tasteful makeup added to that.

"Thank you for meeting me today." Quinn shook her hand and smiled still. Her stomach crawled with anxiety. She'd bought a house before. That wasn't the issue. And she knew a thing or two about cleaning and painting and repairing. She'd even jumped around towns, never one to entirely settle.

No, something else nagged at her. Something she couldn't pin down. A bad feeling.

The problem was Quinn *usually* had bad feelings. Bad feelings directed her life, really. She'd have had a bad feeling if she *didn't* put in an offer. Sight unseen or not, her relationship to 696 Apple Hill Lane had little to do with the many gut feelings from which Quinn often suffered.

Even so, away the two went, up a weed-strewn, broken path to the front door.

Annette fiddled with the lock box that hung clunkily from the brass knob until she emerged victorious with a single tarnished key. "Voila," she said with a flourish, working the key into the lock and knocking her hip into the door to pop it open. "This is the first showing we've had," she admitted as the door finally gave way.

Quinn blinked, then took a breath.

It was worse than she'd expected.

She blinked twice more as the smell hit her square in the nose.

Annette turned to her. "Oh, dear."

2

ANNETTE

The truth about 696 Apple Hill Lane was a carefully preserved secret.

And it had been Annette's main goal to keep it a secret. No way she could broker a transaction if anyone *knew* about what had happened. Even her husband, honest and trustworthy Roman Best, had agreed there.

They wouldn't share details about the house's history until they had a buyer in hand. Someone *genuinely* interested.

As Annette and Quinn stepped into the foyer, Annette couldn't hold back her surprise. The condition was...bad. Without having entered it before now, she could have only surmised *how* bad. This was worse.

Sure, she'd seen the exterior. Every day of her life for the past few years, now. But *wow*. A smile ever plastered to her face, she whipped around to Quinn, who gazed steely eyed about the crowded, dank space. Annette forced herself *not* to plug her nose. "It's a *project*," she sang out.

Quinn must have been breathing through her mouth like Annette.

She had grace. That couldn't be argued. "It's...a big house," Quinn commented as her eyes crept up and over the towering furniture, the piles of *stuff*. They landed back on Annette, and though there might have been trepidation there, she added, "A yard sale might be in order."

Annette's smile brightened earnestly. Quinn Whittle, whoever she was, was *her* kind of gal. "Potential. Potential out the wazoo, I assure you. And yes, you might get a little cash for some of this." She waved her hand around, indicating the mess left behind.

They both took in the sights of the place once again.

The county had come in to assess property value and look for assets to be sold on behalf of the previous owner's estate. Annette hadn't known him—Carl Carlson.

Carl Carlson.

A funny name for an odd, secretive old man. It made sense, in actuality, that he'd have a phony name. Had to be a cover-up, Annette suspected.

Since Mr. Carlson had had no living kin come

forward, they'd leveraged his remaining assets against the debts. At least, this was Annette's weak understanding of the matter, which she'd put together based on the small brokerage fee she and Roman would earn out of the transaction—assuming it came to pass. *Praying* it came to pass. Best on the Block had missed out on a few listings lately. Two in Crabtree Court alone, in fact. The sellers wanted a company that was *more accessible*. This made *no* sense to Annette, and Roman was useless in decoding it, too.

"Comes with the furniture," Annette offered Quinn, running the pad of her index finger along the back of a wood-trimmed Queen Anne sofa. A puff of gray dust dissipated into the air when she rubbed her thumb against it and grimaced inwardly.

Quinn tugged open the drawer of one of two filing cabinets, then shut it and wiped her hand on a little white handkerchief that had materialized from the woman's purse. How quaint. "It's a lot of work," Quinn confessed. Her mouth lay in a flat line.

"But it's a great deal," Annette assured her.

"That's what you said," Quinn replied.

Annette took her cue to explain. "Harbor Hills is one of the safest neighborhoods in Michigan and contends for the same title nationally. We're family-friendly. Property values are higher than average. We recycle here, too."

"I can see that," Quinn answered, lifting a decrepit

newspaper from the top of a leaning stack of others. The editions that sat on the bottom of the tall heap were obviously yellower, like a sad, putrid rainbow of history. A homage to all the things that made the news in little Harbor Hills.

Annette allowed a light chuckle, though she had a strict personal rule about never making fun. Who knew what poor old Carl Carlson was going through? Not her.

They continued the tour, and Annette did her best to point out the redeeming features of the Michigan colonial. Four rooms on the first floor (one bedroom). Four on the second (two bedrooms). The layout was compartmentalized, as were most of the houses built in Harbor Hills at the turn of the century. If it was Harbor Hills Quinn wanted, then she was getting a lot of house in a nice area for a low price.

"So, what brings you to our little hamlet, anyway?" Annette asked as they left the second-floor bath—its clawfoot tub, though overflowing with musty towels and linens, seemed to be of particular interest to Quinn.

She smiled a sad sort of smile. "Family. I, um, I have family nearby."

"In Detroit? Or—" Annette looked her client up and down. The structured black blouse fell to the tops of her thighs. Firm, slender thighs sheathed by fitted, cropped white jeans. She'd fit in on Apple Hill. Better than Carl Carlson, God rest his soul. Annette shook her head at her own awfulness. "Rochester?" she added. Rochester was far more probable than Detroit. Then again, the woman *was* purchasing a *foreclosure*. Annette pursed her lips again at herself. They were compulsive, her judgments. Compulsive.

"My ex is in Birch Harbor. I have some relatives on Heirloom Island, too."

Birch Harbor was a stone's throw from Harbor Hills. In fact, Harbor Hills was named after the little waterfront town on the shores of Lake Huron. Heirloom Island was a small chunk of land that floated just out past Birch Harbor.

"Ex as in ex-husband?" Annette pressed.

"Yes." Quinn's confidence was unshakeable. They paused on the second-floor landing, having examined each of the bedrooms and the bath. "That's how I found out about this house, in fact. I was in Birch Harbor at a family event. Met someone there who knew of a fixer-upper. Something in my budget but... with potential."

Annette nodded. "Right. Judith Carmichael." Judith, who also lived on Apple Hill, had referred Quinn to Annette, apparently. Judith had given no details, however. All she'd said was that she'd met someone interested in a good deal. That was *it*. The rest of the magic would have to come from Annette's showmanship or businesswoman skills or...Quinn's desperateness, perhaps.

"Anyway," Quinn went on, letting out a slow sigh, clearly leading to the fact that the tour was over and there was little more to be added. Little more to be said of Carl Carlson and his hoard. "What's next?"

Annette took this as a good sign and grinned. She propped a thin folder on the bannister as she flipped it open.

Inside, she'd taped the two keys. In each pocket of the folder was tucked the necessary paperwork to satisfy the details of the transaction. However, one loose page hung from a small paperclip in front of the right pocket. "Next," Annette declared with a smile, "you sign here."

Annette bit her lip in anticipation as Quinn's eyes swept the page. A disclosure, required by county ordinance.

The sort of thing that could ruin the sale.

And these days, even if the sale was a softball lobbed to them by First Regional Bank, Annette and Roman Best were just one sale away from *the worst*.

3

JUDE

Since her divorce, Judith Banks had been trying to make a change. Several, in fact.

First, she'd committed to living full time in her Apple Hill home. Gone were the days of tying off at Heirloom Island dock or Birch Harbor marina. Even if she *did* own her own boat, Judith preferred to have both her feet on dry land. Being so close to the chasm that was Lake Huron had started to make her feel as vulnerable as a dinghy, after all. Anyway, it wasn't as if she had much choice. Her ex had gotten the houseboat and the divorce dissolved what extra funds either one of them had access to. In fact, she ought to be thankful to have the pretty two story there in Harbor Hills.

The second change Judith had made was a little less outward. More inward. In addition to reverting to her maiden name and the full-time residency on Apple Hill, she had given up.

Not on *life*, of course. She had given up on all those little things that add stress. The small stuff, as some might say. She'd stopped running a rag along the baseboards every Saturday morning. She opted for the automatic car wash on the corner of Third Avenue and Bunkle Street, rather than a biweekly handwash in her driveway.

And holidays. That was the biggie. Judith Carmichael was one to blow out the holidays, sending Christmas cards to everyone she'd ever met and coordinating the annual Easter egg hunt for the Michigan Foster Society. She made personalized valentines for the folks in Gene's yacht club—a club he only *barely* belonged to. Fourth of July you could find her in red, white, and blue and stars and stripes, with her lawn chair propped in the best spot along Main Street, willing herself to stay awake through the nine o'clock fireworks show.

Judith Banks was *done*.

Done with it all. Now, now that she had her own life to live and her own self to live for, she could opt to let the toilet paper stash get a little low. She could eat cereal for dinner if she wanted. Fall asleep with the television on. Sheesh, she could do anything if she had a mind to!

And that's exactly what she'd do, too.

The third change came on a gust of wind on a bright day in March. The air still nippy, warmth could be found in pockets of sunshine here or there.

"Jude!" a voice called out from somewhere in the vicinity.

Unused to chitchat with the neighbors, she glanced left and right, searching for the source of the error.

She spotted it one driveway over. Beverly Castle, the woman who lived in the house with the blue front door. Blue Beverly was how Judith had come to recall her name.

Judith smiled and waved and then started to correct Beverly. *Judith*, she could say. Or, *Oh, it's Judith. I'm* Judith. *I don't go by nicknames.* Maybe she could even add the "-ith" for Beverly. *Ith!* she could call back, and they could share a laugh and it'd be like Judith was a part of her neighborhood, after all. After all these years of running off with her husband on some excursion somewhere. Leaving, leaving, leaving. All the time. Now she was staying, staying, staying. It might be high time to send cookies around the block or something.

A lightbulb flickered in her mind. This could be her third change. Something to complete her rebirth as a single woman, over the hill but still living in the hills.

An alias.

Well, not quite an alias. More like a nickname.

Jude.

Jude, a divorcée who ate cereal for dinner, ignored the dust on her baseboards, and washed her car only when she felt like it. Oh, and now a full-time member of Apple Hill Lane.

No longer was she Judith Carmichael, wife of Gene Carmichael and town councilwoman of Birch Harbor.

No longer was she Judith Banks, reform school student.

No longer was she Little Judy Banks, the girl from Detroit City with an early history so tragic she buried it six feet under.

4

BEVERLY

"Did you see?" Beverly strode over to her neighbor's house and threw a nod up the street, to the house on the corner of Apple Hill Lane.

Judith Carmichael—if that was still her last name —followed her gaze then looked back. Her white-blond bob swished around her jawline and Beverly was certain something was different about her, even though Beverly didn't know her well. Or, at all. Beverly hadn't been through divorce, but she knew what it was to lose the love of your life. She could read it on others.

That sort of pain changed a woman. But Judith's wasn't the same brand of heartache Beverly had endured. That much was clear.

Judith pressed her purse against her torso protectively like Beverly was dangerous. Maybe she was. But Judith wouldn't know that.

"You mean the car?" Judith asked and blinked through the sunlight.

"The car, sure. The woman who got out of it, too," Beverly replied, craning her neck for a better vantage point. "Annette told me she bought the place sight unseen."

"Oh," Judith answered, returning her focus to Beverly, unfazed, apparently. "Yes. Quinn is her name. Quinn Whittle."

Beverly's eyes widened. "You *know* her?"

Judith shook her head. "No, no. But I met her once. Friend of a friend, you might say. She was looking to buy in the area, and I mentioned a house for sale I knew of."

"Six-nine-six," Beverly said aloud, confirming that Judith Carmichael—prim-and-proper, travel-happy Judith Carmichael—had referred some beautiful stranger to the nearby dump.

"Is that the house number?" Judith asked, glancing over her shoulder. "I wasn't too sure. I only gave her the street name and Annette's phone number. They managed the rest apparently."

"Yes," Beverly confirmed. "Six-nine-six. The Carlson home." It was odd, now, to refer to the place as the Carlson home. Before he passed, Carl Carlson had been as much a ghost as anything else, and everyone knew ghosts couldn't well own homes. And his odd name and bizarre behavior—the obvious hoarding—none of it gelled for Beverly. She let out a sigh. "Well, it'd be nice if someone came in and fixed the place up." Beverly glanced at Judith's house, a beautiful brick colonial not too different from the Carlson abode.

Judith looked beyond Beverly at the Castle house, the one at the end of the cul-de-sac, a little higher up than the others on the street, by virtue of one of many hills in Harbor Hills. "Maybe she could hire you. Seems like you've done a little work."

Beverly looked back at her house, then again to Judith. "It's not much. Just cosmetic."

"The blue door is beautiful." Judith cocked her head like she could see into Beverly's soul.

Beverly dropped her gaze and took a step back, breaking their emerging bond. "Tom wouldn't let me paint it. He liked the natural wood look too much." She winced, her throat closing up. "Well, not *too* much. It's just—well, he didn't like—"

Judith took a step forward and rested her hand on Beverly's shoulder. An awkwardly intimate gesture for two veritable strangers. "I know what you meant," she murmured. "The blue looks nice. I'm sure he'd think so, too."

Smiling and swallowing that pesky sob that never *really* went away, Beverly replied, "My daughter would have *loved* it."

5
___

QUINN

After the tour, Quinn was met with one final surprise.

There was more to 696 Apple Hill Lane than piles of bedsheets and stacks of newspapers and rows of antique furniture.

Carl Carlson, if that even *was* his real name, had not left the house of his own volition.

He had died *in* the home.

According to Annette Best, no one knew about Carl's in-home passing. It was a town secret. Quinn didn't understand why.

Anyway, that was exactly what Annette had to disclose before Quinn signed on the dotted line.

The death made Quinn pause, yes. But her true hesitation had much more to do with *her* than with any external force, such as the ghosts of homeowners past.

She didn't fear other people's demons. Only her own. And that fear—that fear of self, of what she'd have to do to make things work—had her chewing her thumbnail compulsively and tapping the ball of her foot on the hardwood floor.

She swallowed once. Then twice more. Blinked three times.

Then Quinn grabbed the pen, and before she could change her mind, she signed her name and dated the document.

One house farther from her past.

And one town closer to her daughter.

Annette seemed elated and started in with a laundry list of relevant contacts. The water company. Gas. Electric. Telephone, cable, and internet—*You can bundle it all in Harbor Hills!* she'd sung out merrily.

"But you'll probably want to find industrial cleaners. I know I would." Annette pressed a tidy white business card into Quinn's hand. "These people worked miracles for another client of mine." Then, she dropped her voice low. "The grandmother died in the house. On the floor. *Carpet.* She was there for days before they found her." Annette winced appropriately. "Awful," she murmured at last.

That was the point at which Quinn asked, "Do you know exactly what happened to, um, Mr. Carlson?"

Annette shrugged and clicked her tongue. "Not really, no." Then she glanced around. "It was all swept directly away. By whom, I haven't the faintest." She pursed her lips. "I mean, his demise was extremely private, I can tell you that. But if you want to dig up more information, I might know someone who could help." Annette raised an eyebrow and cocked her head.

"I'm not sure I want more information." Quinn blinked and breathed through her nose for the first time since she'd stepped through the front door. She'd finally gone blind to the unpleasant smells of the home. Musty and mildewy and cramped and mottled. The left-behinds of a life poorly lived. Or well lived. It wouldn't hurt, however, to have a point of reference for things. "But who is it?"

"Beverly Castle," Annette answered. "Her number is listed in there"—she tapped the folder—"along with all the rest of us Apple Hillbillies."

Quinn laughed at this as she opened the folder and skimmed the contents. "Harbor Hills is hardly suited to that nickname."

"That's another question for Beverly maybe. She's a newspaper reporter. Or...*was*. I think she's on hiatus. Sabbatical? No, no. Leave. That's it. *Leave.*" Annette clicked her tongue again and drew her lips down into a thin frown. "Husband and daughter passed. Last winter. Terrible tragedy."

Quinn pressed a hand to her mouth. "Oh, my. What happened?"

"Car crash out on Harbor Avenue between here

and Birch Harbor. Terrible, terrible tragedy. An *accident*. As far as that sort of thing can be. Vehicles are loaded weapons. It's why I've got my son in driver's education until he's thirty."

A car-crash. One of Quinn's many ultimate nightmares. The sort that kept her awake at night. The sort that sent her backtracking, ensuring the bump in the road was already roadkill. Not Quinn-kill. She swallowed hard and found a way to bridge the conversation with this woman who was far more normal than she. Someone whom Quinn needed to think of *her* as normal, too.

"My daughter's taking driver's ed this coming school year."

"Daughter?" Annette looked as if she might faint. "You have a teenage *daughter*?"

Quinn flushed. Maybe she shouldn't mention Viviana quite yet. After all, what would this woman think? Annette seemed so...*perfect*. She couldn't possibly understand Quinn's situation.

Still, there was no taking back an admission of that size now.

"Yes. Viviana. She goes by Vivi. She's a sophomore."

"She'll go to Hills High, then." Annette clapped her hands giddily. "I'll have to set her up with Elijah." Her eyes widened and she laughed nervously. "Not like *that*." Annette waved her hands through the air as if to clear out smoke. "I mean for the first day of school. Your Viviana will be in good hands with Elijah. He's...well, he has good friends. He's well liked by teachers. Not necessarily *popular*, but that sort of thing is different in high school these days. You know? I bet you see it with your daughter and her friends."

Quinn just smiled and shrugged, unwilling to disappoint Annette Best of Best on the Block. She felt like too big a person to let down, no matter how kind she was.

"Well, then. You'll let me know if you need anything? I'm just next door." Annette laughed. "And my husband won't mind swinging by if there's any heavy lifting. He wears that sort of thing like a badge of honor. You know men."

Quinn knew *one* man. And that was old news.

She tried to redirect the conversation. "Can you remind me about the HOA?" she began, her face serious as she turned the open folder to Annette. "I'm a little nervous about a homeowners association. I remember you mentioning it on the phone and that there was a nominal fee. Are homeowners association fees ever *nominal*?"

"Oh, right." Annette gave a short nod. "Crabtree Court Homeowners. The community is named for the main drag"—Annette hooked a thumb behind her indicating the crossroad—"since it was the first inroad. We're small, with just five residential lanes running parallel all the way to the back of the community. Beyond that is just woods."

"Right. And it's just fifty dollars a year. Can that be possible?" Quinn's eyes swept through to the front window, inspecting as well as she could the rest of the neighborhood from that limited vantage point.

"We have a board. We have guidelines in place both for new construction and exterior home condition, but"—Annette bounced her head from one shoulder to the other and laughed—"as you can tell we are *lax*. Our biggest point of pride isn't a tidy line of perfectly trimmed grass. Charity projects. You see, we do charity projects. Food drives. Winter coat drives. We take turns shoveling the drives of the elderly residents up the hill. No one on our street quite fits that description yet, however."

"Not even this Carl Carlson character?" Quinn couldn't help but point it out.

"Well, we can't do it without the property owner's permission, you see. Mr. Carlson never answered the door for us. He never came to events. Nothing. There was no way we could help him, I hate to admit."

"Ah." Quinn nodded. She understood this. Refusing people's help and rendering them, in some great irony, helpless. And continuing to remain helpless, too. It was a mess, mental illness. Assuming Carl Carlson had suffered from it.

Quinn certainly did.

She shifted her weight to her left hip and blinked. Then blinked a second time.

A third.

"Speaking of charitable service," she laughed lightly, swallowing hard over a lump that had formed in her throat. Humiliation. "Jobs in the area—do you happen to know of any?"

6

ANNETTE

nnette had promised Quinn she'd get in touch with a few leads, and Annette was a woman of her word. Especially when it came to someone who helped keep her business alive, even in small measure. Even unwittingly.

As soon as she left the poor thing—with great hesitation, too, for Quinn seemed to be entirely alone—Annette got on the phone.

Best on the Block wasn't hiring. In fact, they were downsizing. Or, as her husband, Roman, would say, *unhiring.* Annette didn't like to think about it either which way.

Instead, she focused her brainstorming on whom she knew who *was* hiring. With Best holding the corner on real estate, the only competitors in that industry would be out of town. That fact alone should mean that their company was more successful, but small business ownership was rough no matter what. They seemed to lose more and more listings to bigger regional Realtors.

There were Annette's in-laws who might want to help; they had a construction business, but only one woman worked there, Mrs. Best. And she wasn't going anywhere anytime soon. So, never mind there.

Annette thought of her girlfriends—none were local. Harbor Hills was too tiny a town for most folks to stick around, including Annette's childhood friends.

Her neighbors occurred to her next.

There was Judith Carmichael, and from what Annette could tell, Judith didn't have a job. She was retired or a homemaker or a bit of both, perhaps? Her husband, however, was another matter. He'd been in education, if Annette's memory recalled. Also retired but highly active in the boating community. Or yachting community. Or sailing whatever sort of watersports were fashionable in Birch Harbor. Then again, Annette hadn't seen Gene in months. Where was *he*?

Then there was Shamaine—though Shamaine was only part time on Apple Hill. She had a house in Tucson where she spent the winters. She was around now but doubtful she'd have any leads.

Beverly Castle could be a great contact, in fact. Beverly worked for the *Herald*, and the *Herald* was *the* local source for job listings, naturally. And even the little paper could have a position. Who knew?

Quinn had relayed to Annette that she had a college degree and varied experience. *A little of everything. I'm meticulous. Hardworking, too.* It was clear Quinn was serious, but Annette felt a piece of the puzzle was missing.

"Beverly, hi," Annette cheered into her phone as she settled at her kitchen bar. Not due in the office until later, she may as well get a few chores done. Top of the list was helping the new neighbor. "Question for you."

"Glad you called, Annette, because have *I* got a question for *you*."

"Oh?" Annette laughed. She didn't often speak with Beverly, but she'd always had a warm feeling for her. Particularly lately, in the wake of such tragedy. It was hard not to feel bad about things. "Well, I suppose that's your job, huh?"

Now it was Beverly's turn to laugh, though it came out croaked, strained. Like she hadn't practiced in a while. "The new neighbor—Quinn? Judith Carmichael next door tells me her name is Quinn?" The pretty trill on Quinn's name curled across the line.

Annette smiled. "Yes. Quinn. She's great. She'll fit in around here, I think. She has a"—Annette swallowed the word and rerouted away from the familial detail—"a *request*." There. Straight to the point was smart. Could Beverly sense Annette's dancing around? Her nervousness?

"A request?" Beverly sounded normal. Casual. Curious, actually. Nosey, even? "What sort of *request*?"

"She needs a job, I suppose."

"A *job*."

Annette could practically hear Beverly tapping her French manicure on the tabletop. Did she still wear a French manicure these days?

Maybe not.

Maybe that was the sort of thing a person stopped doing when her world crashed down around her.

"She bought a new house *without a job*?"

Annette had already known—or, at least, had an inkling. Having represented the house and getting an insight into Quinn's financial affairs, she knew that money came from *somewhere*, if not her own work. Her voice dropped on the line. "It's all above board, I assure you. Down payment, I believe. Healthy savings."

"Ah, well, what does she *do*? Or rather, what *can* she do?"

"That, I'm not sure about. She says she's got a degree and experience in a—um—a variety of industries. Maybe something entry-level?"

"At the paper?" Beverly asked. "I don't think we're hiring, but I can pull out the classifieds from today and take a pic to send over. Unless you—subscribe?"

Annette bristled. "Naturally we *subscribe*. I've got

the paper open on the bar now. I'm thumbing through the listings, and there's not much, unless you have special insight?"

"Special insight?" Beverly hummed. "Well, let me ask at the office. Maybe we could use a social media person. I know the editor wants to move into the twenty-first century, I'm just not sure how soon."

"Social media could be great. She's got a teenage daughter, so she probably has good basics." As soon as the sentence was out of her mouth, Annette froze. Oh, how she wished she could suck the words back in with a vacuum cleaner. "I'm sorry, Beverly," Annette murmured.

"Sorry for what? You're right. Teen girls are great with that sort of thing. You know, social media, *texting.*" Her voice was icy.

"I really am sorry, Beverly," Annette repeated. "I—"

"I'll ask my editor."

The phone went dead, and Annette felt a pang in her heart. She hadn't meant to bring it up, of course she hadn't. But Beverly's tragedy was unavoidable. A dark cloud hanging above Apple Hill Lane.

And while not a singular reason to move, surely one more nail in the coffin on the Best family's tenure there.

7

JUDE

A week later saw Judith antsy. Hot, sticky weather kept her indoors, when she ought to be tending her garden.

She had fallen into a slump, that much was true. With her divorce settled, there was no *reason* for the slump. But then, what else had she? She'd spent years on the marriage. *Years* on that man. She'd spent it all.

At least she had the house. And a small score of new friends, though not local.

It might just do to make other new friends who *were* local. Beverly seemed a little interested, after all. And surely the new neighbor, Quinn, would need someone to take her under a wing. It was far easier to navigate a small town or a close-knit community when one had a guide.

Jude could be a guide.

She slid her finger between lace curtains, pulling one back a couple of inches so that she might assess the street.

Just up the bend from her house, which was nestled neatly in the crook of the arm that was Apple Hill, sat the Best house.

On the other side of that was 696, Quinn's house. Six-nine-six was the least sleepy it had ever looked to be. Two different, unfamiliar vehicles sat outside. Though, admittedly, neither one looked to belong to a professional of any degree. A third, Quinn's car, was parked in the drive, not in the garage. Not yet. She had a ways to go, no doubt.

Judith's eyes flicked back to the Best house. Something caught her attention. Something that decidedly did *not* belong in front of Annette and Roman Best's house. A square sign. A familiar, square sign.

No, sirree.

Judith strode to her front door. Liebchen, her Maine coon, curled loop-de-loops around her feet, tripping her up until she was at the door and out, striding with a purpose across the black asphalt and beneath the powerful midday sun.

Just as she was about to cut right onto the white space of sidewalk in front of Annette's—Judith deigned to take the sidewalk the whole way—the rumble of a craggy truck engine came up behind her.

Judith twisted to catch the interloper—no trucks

lived on Apple Hill, to be sure. A man in a classic truck, red and boxy and shiny at every corner, eased past her. Perhaps a house call to Beverly. Or a prospective client for Annette, turning at the end of their street to park the right way, *for once*. Visitors never did that sort of thing—park in the direction of traffic. Being new to someone's house seemed to render people new to the laws of the road, too.

Judith eyed the man behind the wheel. Salt-and-pepper hair. Black sunglasses. Athletic wraparound types, nothing fashionable. That was as much as Judith could make of him before he rolled past her and stopped along the sidewalk between Quinn's and Annette's.

He popped out of the driver's seat, and Judith found herself staring. She swallowed, shook her head, and glanced away.

"Is this the Whittle place?" he called to her, alerting Judith to their close proximity. She'd floated, it seemed, down the sidewalk. Just a few yards away from him and his pretty, big, red truck.

He was tall. Lean. Judith's gaze fell to his left hand, and she pursed her lips, annoyed with herself for where her mind had wandered.

"Pardon?" she asked, pressing a dainty, bare hand to her chest. When was her last manicure? Christmas? For shame.

"The Whittle place. They called an electrician." He

hooked a thumb to his truck, and Judith saw Jericho Brothers scrawled across the door in clean, white script. A metal tool case spanned the width of the bed, and its base fitted to the sides perfectly. "That's me." He took another step up to her, offering his hand across the short distance. "Dean Jericho." He looked bashful. "I know, I know. Family's from Arkansas." He shrugged, and Judith couldn't help but close the gap and take his hand.

Then, she gestured beyond him. "Six-nine-six. That's the Whittle place."

He didn't bother to look.

He already knew where he was headed.

Judith flushed as it occurred to her that she hadn't introduced herself. "I'm—" Her brain short-circuited as her exchange with Beverly from a week before dredged itself up. She flicked a glance at Annette's house and the sign she had set about asking after; Quinn's house beyond, and then back to this stranger who had no need to walk over and introduce himself. Save for the fact that Judith, perhaps, was staring. Had she been? Was she that obvious? She blinked and focused on his kind blue eyes. "I'm *Jude*."

8

BEVERLY

Beverly was late for an appointment—an appointment with her grief counselor, to be specific. There was hardly any shame in seeing a grief counselor. Even six months in. Maybe especially six months in. By this point, the events of the preceding winter were distant enough to be real and still close enough to burn like ice.

A judgment call was in order: text the counselor and say she'd be late, *or* speed.

Beverly knew better. She paused at the bottom of her driveway, a sloping thing on the upside of her property, tucked away from the eyes of her neighbors, as if her car was a precious thing to keep out of the open. Or perhaps, a dangerous thing.

It was.

From where she sat in her driver's seat, she sent a

short, cordial text to the counselor then carefully stowed the phone *deep* in her purse.

When Beverly looked back up, she saw that Judith Carmichael was standing in the road, chatting with a workman, an electrician, from the looks of it.

A little smile danced on Beverly's mouth as she saw the man finally give a nod of his head—or so it appeared from that great distance—then walk up toward Quinn's.

Ah yes, Quinn. The newbie. A woman who had, according to local lore, a teenage daughter. This made no sense to anyone in town or on Apple Hill, naturally. No one had *seen* Quinn's supposed daughter.

But Beverly knew that a woman could have a daughter and the daughter didn't have to be around. She knew it too well.

That said, even if Beverly could relate to a daughterless mother of a teenage girl, she, too, was curious.

Curious enough about Quinn *and* about Judith Carmichael and the electrician that Beverly rolled carefully from her driveway, all but creeping toward Annette's house, where Judith still lingered.

Beverly rolled her window down. "Jude!" she called. Beverly waved, her clacking blue bracelets jangling toward the passenger window.

"Beverly, hi." Judith joined Beverly at her car as she glanced once again after the man.

"New friend?" Beverly teased.

"Oh, no. No, he was looking for Quinn's house."

Beverly raised an eyebrow. There were precisely six homes on Apple Hill. Six-nine-six was the only one in need of work. He wasn't *looking* for Quinn's house. She was certain.

Judith seemed to know this, too, because her cheeks turned rosy and she let a smile curl across her mouth. "I know. He's—oh, you know the type. Blue-collar guys. Always looking for action." Judith rolled her eyes and let the smile slip away.

"When I met Tom, back in college, he worked after-noons as a laborer, you know." It was the first time she'd said his name aloud without a sob crawling up her throat. She didn't mean to contradict Judith's impli-cation, but that's the exact effect Beverly's comment had.

Judith swayed back. "Oh. I..." She smiled thought-fully. "I suppose I never thought of Tom as—"

"As a roughneck? Let me tell you something, Jude." Beverly put her car in park and leaned closer to the passenger side window. "I know Gene is a good provider for you, but there's something to be said about a man who is good with his hands."

Judith recoiled and shook her head.

Beverly couldn't help but cackle. "I'm just joking, Jude. I know you'd never do that. Not to Gene." This was Beverly's way of sussing out the truth. Wasn't it time Judith came clean?

And it worked.

"He's—we're apart. We're...*divorced*, actually."

"Divorced?" Beverly nodded solemnly.

"I was just off to see Annette. Good talking to you, Beverly."

"Jude, wait. Before you go—can you do me a favor?" She didn't pause for an answer. "I'm off to an appointment, but I'd like for us to invite Quinn to join the HOA board, even just as a representative. Could you relay that to her? While you're out and about?" Judith stammered, but Beverly added, "You should come back, too. We could use another active member. Meeting's tomorrow at six. My house. Bring a side."

A knock came at the front door.

Quinn dropped her yellow-rubber-gloved hands to her sides and the left strap of her overalls fell down for the millionth time.

In the kitchen was the plumber, dumbfounded by the plumbing.

In the attic, a carpenter—at least, that's what his Facebook bio said—repairing two rotten beams and not a single one more. Quinn could bear to pay for four hours of his labor and materials.

And now, the electrician. This one could be the most expensive call yet, but something told Quinn it'd be a tough match between the busted circuit board and cracked copper pipes.

"Dean Jericho," he said, falling back half a step as

Quinn pushed the screen door open with her gloved hand.

She waved and blew a puff of air through her lips, lifting wisps of her hair from her forehead for one blissfully cool, painfully fleeting moment. "Quinn. Quinn Whittle. Come right in and make yourself at home." And she meant it, too. Maybe the more other people trampled through the house, the less it would stink. That was Quinn's brand of logic.

Quinn was at the end of her rope. And at the end of the contacts Annette had offered. She'd been spending the nights on the back porch in a sleeping bag. The days she spent sweating through her clothes without consistent running water or electricity. Nothing made sense in her new home. Things worked half the time and in only half of the house.

Still, she was there.

"What can I do ya for, Miss Whittle?" Dean Jericho asked, all but whistling the words. Dean Jericho was the third person who'd been inordinately kind to her that day.

A good omen, to be sure.

"Well, I have changed the lightbulbs throughout this house twice now, and still half of the lights won't switch on. I can't tell if the fridge works, either. Ironically, that lightbulb *does* work, but it feels just cool in there. Not cold."

Dean made a serious face. "I see. Anything spoil?"

Quinn blinked and glanced left and right. "Anything *spoil*?"

"Food in the fridge. Humans are only so-so at testing temperatures, in my estimation."

"Tell that to a mother," Quinn shot back, half joking.

Dean chuckled. "Touché. I suppose you must be one. I'll take your word for it and get to work. But before I do. Anything else?"

"The circuit breaker," Quinn added, gesturing for him to follow her down the hall. "I've flipped the switches and one is stuck. The one to the master." She opened a linen closet door—she'd already divested it of its myriad linens, mostly clean ones.

Dean started there, and this allowed Quinn to feel like she could take a break. She was probably ten percent into cleaning out the house, but the utilities were now under the control of professionals. It was *something*.

She thought about the few bills filed neatly in her wallet. The bank account, only modest. How long would her savings take her through this place? Had she made a mistake?

Snapping off the rubber gloves, Quinn made her way to the industrial-sized bottle of hand sanitizer—the only thing standing between her and sanity, with the water shut off. After three pumps and thirty seconds of lathering, she shook her hands dry then grabbed her phone and opened her texts.

Vivi's most recent sat at the top of the short stack. Just three open conversations. Every other text she'd ever gotten had been deleted. She only ever kept just three in there. Currently, she had messages from Vivi, Matt—Quinn's ex—and Dean Jericho. Now that Dean was here in the flesh, she could save his number and delete his conversation. She opened Vivi's message next.

Texting Vivi felt ridiculous. Their relationship wasn't there yet. Not really.

Quinn tapped out something logical. *Hey. How are you?*

That would come across as forced. Vivi already knew her mother was around.

She backspaced and started over.

What are your plans for the Fourth?

The next prominent holiday. Vivi loved holidays, just like Quinn.

Still, though, she was dancing around the elephant.

Again, she deleted the draft.

I've moved into the house. It's awful.

There. The truth.

Always with Vivi, the truth.

She hit send.

ANNETTE

T he doorbell rang, as if on cue.

Annette expected the visit. She'd been watching out the window some minutes earlier, enjoying the events of midday on Apple Hill Lane. At this time of year, it was more preferable to watch from the comfort of an air-conditioned parlor rather than the sweltering front porch.

She'd only recently returned to her kitchen, where she flapped the paper open and perused real estate listings, a daily habit. Most of the listings were from the heavy hitters out of Detroit, those companies that folks trusted just for their big names. They probably took a lower commission because of volume. They probably promised generous offers from flocks of homebuyers.

She folded the pages back and rose to head to the

door, but Elijah cut her off at the pass. "Got it, Mom!" he called.

Elijah was a good boy. Young man, rather. Tall and sinewy, with dusty brown hair like Annette's and light brown eyes like Roman's. She could see he was destined to be a heartbreaker. Just a little young still. Not immature, but...innocent. At least as far teens went these days.

With a half-eaten apple in one hand, Elijah swung open the door.

Annette peered down the hall to indeed see Judith standing there. From what she knew, Judith was recently divorced. An interesting development in the life of the perfect part-time neighbor. Annette had always looked at Judith and Shamaine as untouch-ables, floating on and off the street with the change in weather, both of them. Judith in the summers to the lake, and Shamaine in the winters to Tucson. Not *real* neighbors. Elegant drifters, too happy and busy to stay put.

But now, Annette realized that Judith had been around for a few months, popping in and out to get the mail, her face more familiar than ever. And maybe a tad different, too.

Annette saw this difference again as she strode to the door, thanking Elijah and dismissing him back to his book or video game or whatever it was he did upstairs when he didn't have his friends over.

"Judith, hi." Annette smiled broadly.

"Jude. Call me Jude." She smiled and gave a shy wave. Annette recognized a bareness in her. Grayish roots. Clean nails, short and square. Milky blue eyes, free of liner. Open and unblinking.

"Oh, right." Annette frowned. "Jude, hi. Is everything okay?"

Judith—Jude—opened and closed her mouth like a bird rooting for a worm.

"The HOA meeting," Annette filled in the blank for her. It was the only relevant thing the two might have shared, and Beverly had already phoned indicating she'd get in touch with Judith about it. "You must be here inquiring about the meeting. I know...*I know*. We've been delinquent. It was Beverly who pushed for a meeting. She wants to plan something for the Fourth of July. A block party. That's her hope, I guess. To put together a block party for the Fourth." Annette opened the door wider and stepped aside. "Come in, please. Roman's at the office today, and I'm home. No showings. Down season, you see," she fibbed.

"Thank you." Judith followed Annette back to the kitchen.

"Coffee? Late for coffee. Hot, too. Iced tea? Arnold Palmer?"

"A water is fine, thanks." Judith clasped her hands.

Annette gave her a once-over. "You're not here about the HOA meeting?"

"Oh, sure. Actually, Beverly stopped me just now, asking to get the new neighbor there, too."

Annette narrowed her gaze. She was shrewder than that. "I know why you're here," she accused with a smirk, realizing the visit had zero to do with Crabtree Court Homeowners.

Jude accepted a glass of water and paled a tad. "The sign?"

"The sign?" Annette asked, shaking her head. "No, *Dean*. Dean Jericho. I noticed your exchange. You must think I referred him."

"No." Jude all but gasped. "Oh, no." A little laugh followed her answer and she washed it all away with a swig of water. "It's the, um, the *sign*. I—was curious, and maybe a little bored, admittedly. Annette, are you *moving*?"

Annette pressed her mouth into a line. "Why? Do you know someone else in the market?"

Jude shrugged then shook her head. "No, I'm sorry. I'm being nosey." She held out the water glass. "I'm sorry, Annette. Forgive me for intruding."

Annette pushed the glass back to her then pointed to the table. "Sit. Sit down. I could really use a confidante right about now."

"Is everything okay?"

"Yes and no. I mean—comparatively, yes. Look at Bev. Look at Quinn—what a mess. And you with your divorce—" Annette glanced up in time to catch Jude wince. "Sorry, it's just...Roman's great. Elijah is happy. But Best is struggling."

"Best?"

"Our company," Annette clarified. "Best on the Block. It seems we lose every listing. Client complaints about high fees, and that's *when* we earn a client. Quinn fell into our lap thanks to *you*, Jude. And the unfortunate circumstances of Carl Carlson," she added.

Jude frowned. "I'm sorry, Annette. I didn't realize. I mean...with a name like Best on the Block, it's a surprise. You've got the right image."

"Image is everything in real estate, too," Annette agreed, downing the last of her coffee—fifth cup of the day. Two too many. "But we can't hack it. Try as we might. And we *do* try. We run social media ads and present open houses. We talk home sellers down and home buyers up. We do *it all*."

"I know what that's like," Jude said, her tone wry and mirthless.

Annette gave her a look, blinked, and rose to exchange her coffee for a water. She needed a clear head. Maybe, somehow, Jude was *onto* something.

She just didn't know it.

JUDE

"So, the HOA meeting," Jude pressed on, "is tomorrow night? Six?"

"At Beverly's, yes," Annette confirmed. By now, she was furiously scribbling onto a notepad, referencing her phone and shooting off texts every so often.

After Annette confessed that they were trying to move—*to a bigger city, somewhere with more opportunity*—she'd grabbed the notepad and her phone and cracked into work furiously.

"Will you still go?" Jude asked innocently. "If you're moving, I mean."

"Well, who *knows* if we're moving." Annette looked up, and there was a new fire in her eyes. An energy. "I mean I can hardly sell other people's homes. Who says I can sell this one?" She cackled then waved a hand.

"Listen, Jude. I'll be at the meeting, of course I will. We've put the house on the market to see if we can get action."

"And if you do, you'll sell?" Jude didn't know Annette, or Roman, or their son well. But for the past decade they'd been neighbors. Maybe longer than that. And now that Jude had the time and focus to give to Apple Hill, she felt a little wounded. Like she was too late.

"*If* we do sell, then we'll take the business to Rochester or Birch Harbor, even. Who knows? But you've given me an idea. And I'm going to run with it."

"I have?" Jude blinked.

Annette set her phone down and dropped the pen, then raised both hands as if to indicate the whole world. "We've done it all. And when you do it *all*, are you really doing *anything at all*?"

Jude wasn't sure she followed.

Seeing this, Annette shook her head. "Best on the Block does it all. I mean we even list hoarding foreclosures." She flung a hand west, toward Quinn's house. "People see our sign on places like that and probably laugh!"

This cut Jude for some reason. When she said she knew what it felt like to *do it all*, she didn't mean she sold out. She didn't mean she was...desperate.

Did she?

"I...I need to go over and invite Quinn. I told

Beverly I would," Jude stammered. She needed to get out of Annette's house and away from the burning sensation that deep down inside, she was exactly like Best on the Block. A phony.

Always had been.

Still was.

Always would be.

Jude or Little Judy or Judith.

It didn't matter what title she gave herself, if she was a loser deep down, pretending otherwise wouldn't change that.

Annette suddenly grabbed Jude's wrist. "Wait," she said, her eyes wild again. "You're retired, right?"

Jude nodded slowly. She'd given her share of time in education. That's how she met Gene. A conference. The two now felt inextricably linked. Teaching and Gene Carmichael. Gene Carmichael and teaching. A sour taste materialized in Jude's mouth.

"And you're here full time. Not like Shamaine. Not anymore," Annette went on.

Again, Jude nodded.

"Maybe you can help me. You're...successful. You're together. People here don't *know* you, but they respect you."

"Help you how?" Jude couldn't figure out where this was going.

"Help me fix Best on the Block," Annette answered, her eyes pleading. "Help me stay."

12

BEVERLY

Hosting the meeting was the perfect distraction.

That's what life had become for Beverly. A series of distractions. Anything to tear her mind away from the trauma. The nightmares. The good dreams that turned out to be nightmares—the ones in which Tom and Kayla were alive. And then Beverly awoke, blurry-eyed and foggy-headed and reached across the bed to tuck her hand beneath Tom's back for a pocket of warmth...and the bed was empty.

And the house was empty.

The sobs came again until she swallowed her morning pill, chasing it with black, sugary coffee. Then, come nine, she'd manage her way to the office, buzzing with caffeine and an empty stomach.

But work was a good distraction, of course.

And so was the HOA meeting, as silly as Beverly took it for.

All HOAs were silly, in Beverly's mind. Made-up rules to make people feel safe. Beverly knew that rules didn't make people safe. Only other people could do that. She knew this fact intimately and painfully and torturedly.

"Ding-dong!" a voice rang through her front screen door. She was wasting her AC by leaving it open, but Tom wasn't around to nag her. What was a few extra bucks these days, anyway?

You can't take it with you.

Beverly smoothed her pastel-blue silk blouse—bought secondhand at Goodwill—then strode to the front door, shaping her mouth into a modest smile. "Is that Annette?"

"The one and only!" Beverly pushed the screen open, and Annette stepped in, carrying on as she usually did. "And have I got the best fruit salad in the world. The secret? Maple syrup."

"Oh!" Beverly took the glass bowl and ushered Annette directly to the parlor.

Each house in the neighborhood of Crabtree Court was outfitted with a formal sitting room, or a parlor. Years back, residents followed the tradition of hosting funerals right there, in the front room of the home, propping the casket open for the wake and setting the food across the hall, in what was now a living room, complete with a television and sound system.

"Your door!" Annette paused and pressed her hand against the painted wood. "Gorgeous shade."

Beverly thanked her on a sigh just as guests started appearing on the front porch.

"I'll let them in!" Annette offered without waiting for Beverly's acknowledgment, and Beverly just had to smile. This was Annette. So comfortable in other people's homes. Here was Beverly, not even comfortable in her *own* home.

Soon enough, enough residents had arrived that they could begin.

In attendance were Beverly, Annette, Judith, Quinn, and Shamaine—the Apple Hill crew. Two from Pine Tree Place—Mrs. Burkle and Mr. Gladstone. And one from Dogwood Drive—Mrs. Cranefeld.

Once drinks and food were duly doled out, Mrs. Burkle suggested they begin.

They first went over the budget, which was plump since they hadn't taken on any projects lately. Mrs. Burkle prattled about everything except the HOA for some time, reminding Beverly exactly why she *used* to dread these meetings. Lately, though, the mindless chatter was welcome. And now that folks had stopped bringing up Tom and Kayla, Beverly was content to get lost in the seemingly trivial matters of her neighbors.

"And, Quinn, dear, tell us all about *you*," Mrs. Cranefeld interjected.

Beverly saw Quinn's lips purse. According to Jude, she hadn't been overly interested in joining the meeting. She looked worn down.

Still, Quinn answered, "Well, I finally got running water to all the faucets, which means I took my first full shower in a week."

The others laughed politely, as if it was the polite thing to laugh at Quinn's expense.

"Quinn," Beverly hissed good naturedly, "you could have showered here."

"I didn't know it was that bad." Annette smirked as though the newcomer might be exaggerating.

"Oh, it's quite bad. The plumber and electrician agreed that it was almost unimaginable that anyone had been living there for quite some time." She popped a piece of watermelon in her mouth, chewed it, swallowed, then added, "At least, assuming whoever lived there was using the modern utilities. Water, lights, heat, and air."

"I don't ever recall seeing smoke puff out the chimney, come to think of it," Shamaine offered.

"Just how long ago did Mr. Carlson pass, Annette?" Mr. Gladstone asked, as though Annette was Queen of Crabtree Court. She sort of was.

Annette sucked in a breath and shook her head

before stealing a glance at Beverly. "I think it was—it was last winter, if I recall."

"Did he take himself to the hospital?" Shamaine asked. "Or, what exactly happened? I mean...I was wintering in Tucson." Only Shamaine Lavigne used *winter* as a verb. If Beverly weren't mentally transported to that awful time, she'd have smiled at Shamaine and her Shamaine-isms. But here she was, in a meeting that was supposed to be about anything *other* than last winter, and they were talking about exactly that.

"I'll go refresh our drinks," she offered, standing and picking up the galvanized metal serving tray with which to collect their glasses.

"Didn't the *Herald* run something on it?" Mr. Gladstone asked after Beverly had taken his half-empty lemonade.

"Hm?" She feigned confusion and tried to sashay off, but the man was either a social hermit or a jerk. Who knew which?

"You work for the paper, Beverly. Didn't the paper run a story on Carl Carlson?"

At his insistence on an answer, she shook her head firmly and left the room.

But she wasn't all the way out before she heard Annette murmur, "There was a bigger story that week."

13

QUINN

She was out of her element in the HOA meeting and particularly so once the banter turned to her own house.

Whoever the Carl Carlson character was who'd lived there before clearly had a reputation. The odd thing was that no one had ever seen him. Heard from him. No one *knew* him.

Quinn couldn't decide if it was a point of interest for her or a point of concern. For now, she was more focused on getting the house in good enough shape to bring Vivi there. Yes, that was it. She had her goal, but still she needed to apply a timeline.

Jude cleared her throat, dragging the group's attention to her. "Annette mentioned a block party?"

"Oh, right!" Annette jumped on this nugget and

ran with it. "A block party. Beverly? Did you want to get into it?"

Quinn watched as Beverly formed a measured response. Something about Beverly felt familiar. Not her looks—her warm chestnut hair or honey-colored eyes. She had a slight build to match her unassuming face, but she was put-together. Pretty and stylish, as though she spent an inordinate amount of time preparing herself for each day.

Quinn knew what it was like to prepare herself for the day. The rituals. The exhaustion, too. Was that it? Behind Beverly's meticulous exterior...was it *exhaustion*?

"Right, well, I thought it might be nice for us to form a new tradition, of sorts," Beverly began, glancing around the room.

"Everyone goes to Main Street for the Fourth. That's where the *party* is," Annette pointed out, her lips curling mischievously.

One of the others—Quinn couldn't recall all their names quite yet—chimed in. "Judith, don't you coordinate the Main Street event? What, you even have a name, right?"

Judith—or Jude, as she'd corrected the others—answered, "Freedom on Main Street, that's right." She said it with a half sigh, her typical polite-if-curt smile entirely absent.

"What?" Annette asked. "You're not putting it on or something?" Quinn had quickly learned that Annette tried hard to read people. Whether she was *right* in her readings remained to be seen. But she sure gave it a go. She...*cared*. Too much? Quinn wasn't sure. If it weren't for the three visits so far, it might not have even stood out to her yet. But Annette had "popped over" with cookies, lemonade, and a full-blown welcome basket on those separate occasions, each time prying a tad more than the previous.

"Oh, I don't know," Jude answered.

"It's less than a month out. Have you been in touch with the council?" Annette pressed her.

Quinn felt the rumble of discomfort in her stomach. She took a small sip of her drink, willing it to pass. She had grown to fear confrontation—her own and others'. This had come from Vivi, naturally. Not *Vivi*. Quinn cursed herself silently for the thought. The fear of confrontation hadn't come from *Vivi*, it had come from Quinn's poor attempt at *parenting* Vivi. All that Vivi was or wasn't had everything to do with all that Quinn was or *wasn't*.

Jude shrugged. "Sure, I have. I mean, the event practically runs itself. We don't gear up until the week of. We have time."

"Then we have time to make a change," Annette replied.

"Jude," Beverly went on, "do you think you might be willing to start a *new* tradition?"

"And betray the rest of the town?" one of the other neighbors asked, guilt coating her voice.

"I never said betray the rest of the town," Beverly defended herself. "I just wonder if she might be willing to focus her talents even more locally for once. Just this year, even. To get us started. Or maybe you could consult for us."

"It's a block party," Annette spat flatly then laughed at herself. "Hiring a consultant for a *block* party? How HOA *are* we?" She rolled her eyes. "Jude, you give us some direction, and we can pitch in at the Harbor Hills event in return." Quinn saw Annette wink directly at Beverly. "A midday block party on Apple Hill, and then the usual festivities on Main."

Jude shrugged a second time and tucked a strand of her hair behind her ear. Quinn saw glimmers of gray peek through the neat coif. Something was *off* about Jude. The first time Quinn met her—out in Birch Harbor—she was a different woman. Icy and severe and *elegant*.

Now, she looked...normal?

"Apple Pie on Apple Hill," Jude answered, a small grin forming on her lips. "I'm in."

Quinn smiled along with the others, who dove into Jude's idea with enthusiasm. Then, she felt a buzz at her thigh. Her phone.

Discreetly, she reached into her small purse and removed it, studying the screen.

It was Vivi. Warmth flooded Quinn's body, but it left just as quickly. Confusion took its place. Ice-cold, heart-numbing confusion.

I still can't believe you moved next door to a murderer.

14

ANNETTE

"Apple Pie on Apple Hill it is!" Annette declared at the end of their planning session. The idea was bittersweet. On the one hand, it'd be nice to leave the street on a high note.

On the other hand, it'd be hard to leave on a high note.

Of course, that was *if* they could find a buyer for their house. The odds were against them, anyway. Who knew?

After the meeting, Annette walked home to find Elijah and Roman lounging in front of the television.

"What are your plans for tomorrow, Elijah?" she asked, willing away the nag in her tone.

He shrugged and tugged his phone from his pocket.

"You could come down to the office," Roman suggested. "Pitch in."

Annette all but rolled her eyes. There was nothing for a teen boy to do at their real estate office. If they were busy, maybe he could stake signs or remove them. But they weren't—so...

"What if you go next door?" Annette suggested, falling onto the couch between her boys and stealing the remote from Roman's thigh.

"Next door?" It wasn't quite a moan or a groan, but Elijah's tone was enough to put Annette's nerves on edge.

"You need to do more than lounge around the house," she replied.

Roman, as usual, came to his son's defense. "He's got a part-time job, Ann."

Elijah lifeguarded for the community pool. Three days a week. Six-hour shifts. Girls in bikinis. It hardly counted.

"Which leaves another part of his time, right?" she pointed out.

"Mom." This time, Elijah *did* groan.

"Are you talking about Judith Carmichael's?" Roman asked, sliding his gaze from the television to Annette.

She caught his inflection, ignored it, and answered Elijah. "I'm talking about Quinn, obviously. That house is more than she can handle."

"*Or* afford," Roman pointed out. "Just like *this* house is more than *we* can afford. What is it with Crabtree Court and people who live above their means?" Roman pushed up from the sofa. This time, *he* ignored *Annette*. "I'm going to bed. I'm tired."

"Tired from what? Sitting at the office staring at the phone?" She had taken it too far. She knew she had. Especially in front of Elijah. But he was a good boy, and he took his cue.

"I'll go next door tomorrow, Mom." Then he stood, too, and left the room.

It was now only Roman and Annette, facing each other and their problems alone. A commercial for a tire sale blared behind them.

"Why do you do that?" Roman asked.

"Do what?" Annette shot back. "Point out the obvious?"

"Exactly," Roman answered.

"Why do *you*?" She pushed her fingers through her hair then drew them back to massage her temples. "Sorry. I'm sorry, Roman. I just—"

"You don't want to move. I know. Neither do I."

"Neither does Elijah," she added.

"I know." Her husband sighed and fell back into the sofa, grabbing Annette's hand and tugging her down with him.

She let him, falling into his side as he wrapped her

in his arms and buried his head in her hair. "I'm sorry, Annie," he whispered.

A single tear formed along her lash line. Humiliation. Disappointment. General sadness. Who knew what else? "Me, too," she murmured back.

Roman kissed the top of her head and pulled away. "It's not your fault that our business is failing."

"It's as much mine as yours. We're a team, remember?" Annette swallowed, scared to ask the next logical question. "Roman," she started, willing away a second tear, the tear that would release the floodgates and turn her from pitiful to pathetic. "Where do we go from here?"

He squeezed his eyes shut and rubbed a knuckle into each one. "We don't give up. We just...we just keep trying."

But she shook her head. It was a bad answer. Wrong. "When *do* we give up, Roman?"

Frowning deeply, Roman answered, "Never. We never give up."

Wrong again.

"We can't afford our mortgage, Roman."

"That doesn't mean we change our business, Annette. This was our *dream*."

Now, that was true. Selling houses still *was* Annette's dream. Roman's as well. They both had an interest in sales, for starters. But more than that, they both loved...*houses*. Big, small, old, new. Before they had Elijah, they'd sometimes drive around looking for For Sale signs, peeking in windows and testing back doors. Sheesh, Roman *proposed* to Annette in one such empty property. They were traveling—Maine for a realty convention. One day, after five back-to-back sessions, they left the conference center and headed back to their hotel abuzz, wondering if they ought to lay down roots there, in that tiny foreign town. Hamlet Hollow was the name of it. They came across a Short Sale sign on a decrepit Victorian at the end of an otherwise houseless wooded lane.

The front door had no lock—had no *doorknob*. Whoever was in charge of the place had clearly given it no nevermind. They slipped in, admiring the original parquet floors, the curling banisters and narrow halls; and it was *there*, as they trespassed, that Roman had dropped to a knee, grabbed Annette's hand, and asked if she'd sneak into empty houses with him for the rest of their lives.

She said yes, naturally, and she'd say it again now, almost twenty years later.

"Something's gotta give, Ro," she whispered, lacing her fingers into his.

"That's why we're selling."

"And then what? What happens next?" She looked up at him. "Assuming we *do* find a buyer?"

Roman blew air through his lips and avoided eye

contact. Annette knew he was going to say something she didn't want to hear.

And he did.

"We downsize."

"You mean downgrade." A sour taste pooled in her mouth. Annette was no snob, really. She'd grown up with a tough family—divorced parents who cared more about alimony and child support than ballet class tuition or wholesome suppers. Fast food was the norm. Christmas gifts were knock-off toys. Never the *real* thing. Not in her childhood home.

With Roman, she'd demanded the real thing. And he'd secured it for her. They'd secured it *together*. But the last few years were trending in the opposite direction. Could Annette stand to be anything other than what she'd grown to cling to? That perfect working mother who could balance it all and still find time to trim the rosebushes? Hire a team of cleaners for in-home parties? Use her own house for business cocktail parties where *no doubt* people would steal photographs of her elegant foyer, her tasteful gourmet kitchen—all those trappings of a *successful Realtor*. A successful *woman*.

Roman brought her hand to his lips, pressing it there and then looking at her, holding her gaze. "I mean live in a way that allows us to keep doing what we love."

"Selling houses," Annette murmured back. "We could go to a different city. Open a new business."

"Elijah has three more years of school. You want to rip him away from his friends?" Roman shook his head. "Not gonna happen."

"Okay then. We downgrade."

"Down*size*," Roman corrected.

Annette smirked. "What*ever*." He always made her feel twenty again. "Anyway, we're going to need a buyer first."

"Know of anyone who can afford to live on the best street in Michigan?"

15

JUDE

Jude had promised Annette she'd come over for coffee the next day. The woman sounded desperate.

Now, here she was, nursing a warm mug with hazelnut-flavored creamer. Delicious.

"Remember how I asked you to help me stay?" Annette stirred sugar into her drink and tapped the spoon on the rim before joining Jude at the breakfast bar.

"Yes," Jude answered, nodding slowly.

"Well, we aren't staying anymore. Not on Apple Hill."

Jude frowned. "You're moving, then?"

"Well..." Annette sort of shimmied on her side of the granite countertop. "We have to sell this place, yes. It's more house than we need, *truly*. However, leaving

Harbor Hills? Not a chance. Roman and I had a long talk. There's Elijah to think of. And Roman is convinced the market will turn around. He thinks we can resurrect our business. But for now, we need to cut the bills down to size and ensure that this house retains every last *ounce* of property value it deserves."

"I'm not sure how to help with that. I'm in a pinch, myself," Jude confessed. Divorced, reduced to the house that she wasn't sure she could afford to begin with, and now living on a fixed income without alimony—she was probably in worse shape than Annette. In fact, Jude herself was headed back to the classroom. She said as much. "I've actually taken up with Hills High. The English department needed a sophomore literature teacher."

"Hills High?" Annette gasped, alarmed, apparently, by this revelation. "You're...coming out of retirement? Why?"

"Help make ends meet, just like you."

Annette's brow line softened. She cocked her head. "Would you look at us? The residents of Apple Hill have fallen apart. First Beverly, the poor thing. Now financial stress."

Jude shrugged and offered a simple smile. "Life."

"Life," Annette echoed.

Thinking better of diluting Beverly's loss to one word, she added, "I'd rather get divorced and go back to work than lose a loved one, though. I don't know how she does it." Jude glanced down the hall toward the front door, trying to make out Beverly's corner of the street from that distance. She could not.

"God bless her," Annette agreed. "That's why I'm all about this block party, though. Beverly needs every distraction she can get. She's back to work, you know, which is *great*."

"That is good, yes. Good for Beverly. And I think she's trying to take Quinn in. As a project, sort of."

"Every woman needs a project. And every woman *is* a project," Annette went on, "which brings me to my favor."

"All right." Jude took another draw of her drink, savoring the sweetness before swallowing and meeting Annette's stare.

"This favor isn't only for *me*, though," Annette continued, holding Jude's gaze so intensely that she was afraid to blink.

"Okay." Jude nodded.

"The block party, you see, it's three weeks out."

"Right. I told Beverly I'd organize, if that's what you're asking. But that's the first and last. My party-planning days are over after that."

Annette frowned. "What about Freedom on Main?"

"I quit. I'm not doing it anymore."

"Because of teaching?"

"No," Jude said simply. "Because I don't want to. I need a break from all that jazz."

"Oh, right." Annette blinked. "Well, that's not exactly what I was asking about."

Jude waited.

Annette finished, "Quinn's house. You see, if we are going to have a block party on Apple Hill, I think she'd like to have it in better shape by then. After all, the whole community is invited. It's not just *us*. People's eyes will be on every house on this street. Mine, too."

Jude considered this. Classic Annette. Always about how things looked on the outside. Never mind the turmoil raging within. Jude wondered what fueled the woman's need to have things *just so* all the time. All the time. "I doubt she wants to rush that big of a job. She has a lot of work. It's not as if she can throw on a can of paint and brush her hands off."

"No, no. You're right. You see, though, the HOA hasn't taken on a charitable project in over a year. Why don't we...why don't we take on 696?"

THE NEXT LOGICAL STEP, naturally, was to see about Quinn. See how she was getting on. Apparently, Annette and Roman had already talked to Elijah about this effort, because he found his way down the stairs shortly after Jude agreed with Annette. Worn jeans and a battered tee made him look different than usual. Elijah was an inside sort of boy. Quiet and academic, with glasses and a neat haircut. Now, in work clothes, he came across with an edge. Jude immediately thought about Viviana Fiorillo but just as soon banished the image. No way would Vivi find her way up to Harbor Hills.

Not yet.

Not if Jude had that girl pegged.

16

BEVERLY

Summer at the *Herald* was the hot season. Crime was up—though not necessarily in Harbor Hills; town events stacked up on the weekends, and the changeover to the new fiscal year typically drew out some drama *somewhere*.

This year, the big story to capture readers across the days of the week happened to do with Hills High and its high turnover rates. Something in the water, according to rumor. As such, Forrest Jericho, Beverly's editor, was all ears when she came to him with the idea to bring someone new on board.

It didn't hurt that the new person in question was an eligible bachelorette. The Jericho men had a local reputation. Forrest for being a heartbreaker, and his brother Dean for being brokenhearted.

Beverly wasn't interested in Forrest's interest,

however. She said as much, swatting away his too-personal questions.

"All you need to know, Forrest, is that she's willing to work. Work hard, too."

"Wait a minute, now." He stopped her, one hand on his hip, the other loosening his tie at the neck. Forrest Jericho never kept his tie tight past noon. "Does she have experience in social media? Just because someone shares Facebook memes that doesn't make her an expert."

"All I know is that she's hoping to make a home here," Beverly argued, feeling itchy. She regretted putting her neck out for Quinn. Sure, she'd been happy to help the woman...but vouching for her? It was an iffy scenario.

Didn't matter, though. Beverly knew she was golden. Golden at the *Herald* and golden in Harbor Hills. One of the benefits of personal tragedy was that no one was going to make more trouble if they could help it. Not in a small town like Harbor Hills, at least. And not at the heart of the community, the *Herald*. If Forrest Jericho fired Beverly for referring a bad egg, the town would protest and see to it that the *Herald* fell by the wayside along *Life Magazine* and every other dead print.

So, the worst that could come from all this was Quinn wouldn't get the job. The best that could come? Beverly helped someone.

"Give her a call and tell her to come in for an interview," Forrest said, giving Beverly a nod and a half smile and turning back toward his office. He twisted to her before stepping through the door. "This afternoon."

Beverly's chest swelled a bit, and she wondered if another panic attack was coming on.

She took a deep breath, and the sensation ebbed. She realized it wasn't a panic attack, no.

It was the first time, in a long time, that she had a *good feeling*.

A borderline happy feeling.

"QUINN, hi. It's...Beverly. Beverly Castle, your neighbor." Beverly cradled her cell phone between her ear and shoulder as she moved files and books on her desk, clearing space on her at-a-glance calendar.

"Hi!" Quinn's voice was light and bright, and that almost-happy feeling returned to Beverly's insides, making her uncomfortable and squishy. "How are you?"

"I'm...I'm okay." Beverly never admitted to being *good* or *well*. She couldn't imagine being either *good* or *well* and definitely not *great!* ever again. But she could be okay. At least in this moment. "I'm calling about the gig at the paper I mentioned. Social media?"

Beverly could hear Quinn suck in a breath and let it out. "Yes, sure. I remember."

"My boss—my editor, that is—he'd love to talk to you. See what your experience is. Your goals. Do you think you could make it this afternoon?" Beverly found herself biting her lower lip in anticipation. As if this little setup somehow mattered. In the grand scheme of things, it didn't, she knew.

Or did it?

"Yes! What time? I'll get ready now. I have a few workers here—but I can slip away. Easy."

"We're here until five, but the sooner you can come in the better, I think. If possible."

"Give me an hour," Quinn promised.

"I'll tell Forrest."

"Forrest, got it," Quinn answered. "He's the...owner?"

"Editor, but he owns the paper, too. Forrest Jericho. And he's looking for a social media manager."

"Forrest Jericho," Quinn murmured. "Got it. See you in an hour. And Beverly?"

"Yes?"

"Thank you."

Beaming inwardly, Beverly got off the line and penciled Quinn into her calendar as if she was the secretary instead of a senior reporter. Sometimes, she felt like a secretary. It was easier to be a secretary. No pressure. No big story waiting in the bushes. No leads to follow. No rumors to untangle. No rumors to find herself at the center of, either.

Then again, being a senior reporter, it was also in her power to direct the town's conversation. And if she directed the town's conversation, then she could *redirect* their attention. News about Hills High turnover was growing stale. They'd need another morsel to glob onto soon.

Something occurred to her.

Beverly pushed away from her desk and swung her upper torso into the doorframe of Forrest's office. "I think I have an idea for a story. Quinn might be able to help us, in fact. It's something...old."

He replied without looking up from his computer. "Old doesn't sell. *New*. That's why it's called the *news*, remember, Bev?"

Beverly shook off the nickname and narrowed her gaze. "Well, this is old *and* new. Do you know anything about Carl Carlson?"

17

QUINN

Her conversation with Vivi had turned short. Quinn had no idea what her daughter meant. She lived next door to a murderer? Could that be...Annette?

Not a chance. Annette was the most normal. Cheerful. Happy. Not the killing type.

Judith? This only made more sense by virtue of the fact that Vivi *knew* Judith. At least a little. But who would Judith have murdered? She divorced her husband. She didn't kill him. And beyond that, Judith was...bored-acting.

Beverly...obviously Beverly was the closest of the three to death. She'd lost two people close to her. But murdered them? No way.

Once Quinn had reasoned through Vivi's accusa-

tion, she clicked her phone off, deciding to be the mom
instead of the gossip that Vivi tried to make her into.

THE NEXT DAY, she got a call from Beverly. A good
distraction from Vivi's fearmongering *and* from living
at the threshold of hell.

She dashed around the house giddily because,
well, this was what she *needed* in order to stick around.
And anyway, she wasn't sure what to do with herself. If
she were back in her condo, she'd have scrubbed
dishes until her hands were raw. Now, though, there
was too much to tackle. So instead, she scrubbed her
body in a hot shower. Hard and rough and three times
through. She got out, red-skinned and raw, and *ready*.

Two showers in as many days had Quinn feeling
like nothing short of a queen. That, plus makeup, a
fresh outfit, and a blowout? There's no way she
wouldn't get the job. Not if this Forrest Jericho character had a heartbeat.

She tracked down the electrician, another idea
dawning on her. "Um, *Dean*?" she asked, as he squatted
near a charred outlet. A small electrical fire, probably.
Ages old, maybe.

He swiveled. "Yes, ma'am?" His good manners were
hard to ignore, and Quinn flushed. Dean was older

than her by a decade or more, but he was a good-looking guy.

"Your company name—Jericho, right?"

"That's right. Jericho Brothers. It's me and Rusty."

"Oh, Rusty." Quinn nodded. "I have a job interview at the paper in town, and the supervisor there, I think he's a Jericho?" Couldn't hurt to gain a little traction with the locals, even if it was only half hour ahead of her meeting.

Dean blew out a sigh. "That'd be Forrest."

Quinn was uncertain of his tone, until Dean stood, brushed his hands together and gave her a wide grin. "You're gonna love Forrest."

18

ANNETTE

They tromped up to 696, Annette in the lead, and made their way through towers of old furniture and lumpy trash bags that all but steamed with the smells and horrors of Carl Carlson, God rest his soul.

Annette and Jude ascended the steps, but Elijah lingered at the bottom, inspecting what looked to be an old—very old—IV machine.

"Elijah," Annette hissed. "Get up here."

He shrugged and joined his mother, whispering, "That's weird," as he hooked a thumb back toward the antiquated medical equipment.

"My mother was on in-home dialysis for *years*," Annette explained to Jude. She flicked a look at Elijah. "Do you remember?" She clicked her tongue. "No, probably not. Too young." Annette swallowed down the pain and threw her shoulders back before raising her finger toward the doorbell.

She stopped short. The doorbell, a cheap plastic circle encased by a brass-colored plastic frame, bobbed out from its place next to the door. It protruded, rather securely, from a single, buoyant wire.

Annette pressed her mouth in a line. Jude stepped forward and lifted her hand to knock on the wood siding, but the door swung open just before she made contact.

The air sucked them all closer to the screen door, now the only divider between Quinn and her visitors.

She looked even prettier than she had the evening before at the HOA meeting, practically glowing through the dingy mesh. She pushed the screen carefully toward them, and all three stepped back.

Her white-blond hair all but floated around her, blown in big rolls, high on her head but not Texas high. More like...California high. Her eyes beamed blue inside more makeup than Annette had yet to see her wear. Her outfit—a pristine red blouse and those formfitting white jeans from their first meeting—gave way to tasteful tan espadrilles, adding to her already notable height.

Annette thought she heard Elijah take a gulp.

"Well, hi," Quinn said, her hand still holding open the screen. A black purse was slung over one shoulder, and it occurred to Annette that, as beautiful as Quinn was and as stylish, her purse didn't match her shoes. In fact, she wore no two colors the same. And yet...she was the image of perfection. *Note to self*, Annette thought, *matching is so last season.*

"Hi." Annette smiled warmly. "I hope we aren't catching you at a bad time?"

Quinn's smile wobbled. "Actually, I'm just headed out to meet Beverly. Well, Beverly's *boss*." She grinned again, softly, at Annette. "Thanks to *you*, I suspect."

"That's right!" Annette's eyes widened. "The *Herald*. So, they *are* hiring. Wonderful!"

"We'd better not get in your way," Jude added.

"Right," Annette agreed. "We just came over to offer help." She glanced at Elijah. "Mainly to offer up this boy here to help you. But we're looking for something to do, anyway."

"That's so sweet," Quinn cooed, cocking her head and offering a motherly look at Elijah. "You must be—"

"Elijah," he croaked then cleared his throat. "I'm Elijah."

"And you're taking driver's ed," Quinn added.

Annette winced. She knew how this would turn out. She could feel Elijah's subdermal seething, but he was a good boy. "That's right. I'll be a sophomore, so, yeah. Driver's ed."

"My daughter is your same age," Quinn said confidently. Annette felt a tonal shift, but she wasn't sure why.

"That's right," Jude said easily. "Vivian?"

"Viviana," Quinn corrected. "She goes by Vivi."

"And when do we get to meet this Vivi?" Annette asked warmly. Cloyingly, perhaps.

Quinn blinked, her smile fading for a second time. "Soon," she said. "Anyway, thank you, all three of you, for coming over. I'd love to have company, of course. Maybe later?"

"We'll come back," Jude answered, taking a step backward. "Just let us know when's a good time."

"Yes," Annette agreed readily. "And let us know when Vivi gets here, too." She felt Elijah's stare on her but ignored it, instead doubling down. "I'm on the PTSO, and I'd be happy to help you get her registered."

"Oh." Quinn closed the wooden door behind her and stepped over the threshold, joining them awkwardly on the front porch. "She—um...Vivi might not go to the local high school."

"What?" Annette looked at Jude, whose face remained impassive. Elijah, beyond, shifted his weight and shoved his hands into his pockets. Nervous. Irritated. Both. "Hills High is the only secondary school in Harbor Hills. We don't have private or charter here." She raised an eyebrow.

"Sorry, can we chat later? I'd hate to be late for this," Quinn replied as politely as could be.

Annette was ashamed of herself. "Oh, of *course*. Of *course*! You go. Go, go, go!"

They all but skipped down the steps together, heading in generally the same direction as Quinn veered toward her vehicle and the other three toward the sidewalk.

Quinn waved them off, and Annette called back a hearty good luck.

It wasn't until they were back at her house that she asked Jude what she knew about Vivi.

Jude frowned. "Vivi's why Quinn moved here."

"What do you mean? If that's so, then why isn't Vivi *here*? Why isn't she going to Hills High?"

Shrugging, Jude answered, "Maybe she'll change her mind. Who knows? Teen girls are tough. I know that better than most. Especially ones who went to St. Mary's on Heirloom Island."

"She went to the Catholic school, then?" Annette brightened at this nugget. "She must be beautiful *and* smart, then?"

It was Elijah's turn to jump in, catching both the women off guard. "I thought that was, like, an alt school or something."

Annette looked at Jude. "An alt school?" She looked back at her son. "You mean a boarding school? A school for troubled girls or something?" She laughed at the idea—so antiquated—of a private Catholic school that took in wayward youth. It was...quaint, actually.

"Yes, in fact. It used to be just that," Jude answered. "When I was there."

"When you taught there?" Annette asked.

"No. When I went there."

19

JUDE

Jude wasn't entirely ready to explain herself—her past, that was. So, when Annette blinked compulsively, she dismissed the matter.

"Years ago. Things were different in the world then." She smiled at Elijah. "Vivi is just as beautiful as her mother."

"What's the story on Vivi's father?" Annette asked. "Quinn's ex?"

Elijah, to his credit, slunk out of the room and away from the conversation.

Jude gave Annette a pointed look. "He's in Birch Harbor."

"Yes, she told me. Are they...on good terms?"

Jude considered this. In truth, she wasn't sure. All she knew was what she'd seen in that one fleeting moment in Birch Harbor. Quinn had been nervous then, just as she appeared generally nervous now. Nervous, but put-together. A surprising combination. "I don't know much more than that. I don't know Quinn at all. Matt—her ex, that is—he's nice enough. Respected around town. He's with someone else now. Vivi even has stepsisters or something. Or one stepsister, I think. No, wait. Stepbrothers? Who knows? It's complicated, to be sure. Birch Harbor is one big family of people. Part of the reason I was happy to slip away."

"Is everything *resolved*?" Annette dropped her voice on the last word, indicating she meant the divorce and all the drama that swirled around that.

Jude nodded assuredly. "Of course. It's a closed chapter. Or, perhaps, a closed *book*. A saga, you might say." She couldn't help but grin. "I'm happy to be here now. Away from all of that."

"Good for you, Jude. *Good for you*." Annette gave her a gritty look and swung a fist across her own chest. A *We can do it!* sort of gesture.

"Speaking of being *here*..." Jude pressed, aware that she and Annette had formed a quick comfortability between each other of late. "What about you?"

"What about me?"

"Any nibbles on the house?" Jude asked.

Annette snorted. "Since yesterday? No. But that's fine. Remember, my eye is on the block party. If we can pull together a smashing event complete with a street lined in gorgeous houses, I bet I can make a move, so to speak."

"And where *will* you move?" Jude asked, accepting a glass of lemonade. She really shouldn't, what with all the sugar. And anyway, she'd better get back home. She had lists to write up for the party. And ideas to brainstorm for helping Quinn. Jude was officially wrapped up in the goings-on of Apple Hill Lane. She took a slow sip, savoring the sweet-and-tart liquid.

Annette shrugged. "Who knows? Hopefully nearby. Maybe even another home in Crabtree Court. Something a little more manageable. Now that we're nearly empty-nesters, we really don't *need* a third bedroom, of course."

"True." Jude thought of her own house—three bedrooms, two baths. Complete with everything a would-be mother would need to house a family of four —or even five. Six, if her would-be kids didn't mind sharing rooms. She wouldn't have as a child, that was certain. She blinked away the thought of her own childhood and refocused on her lemonade, drinking half before offering the glass back to Annette. "I've got to get home. Lots to do on both of these projects."

"Right." Annette took the glass and walked Jude to the door.

When they got there, they watched together as a truck dragged itself around the cul-de-sac in a slow, looping fashion, stopping just behind the Jericho

Brothers truck that straddled the property line between Quinn's and Annette's.

"Who's *that*?" Annette asked, pushing her screen door to its limit and stepping out behind Jude.

Jude squinted through the daylight until her gaze fell on the tall, dark-haired man who unfolded himself from the driver's seat.

He shielded his eyes from the sun and looked at the house next to Annette's, then rounded the hood of his truck and opened the passenger door.

Out hopped a wisp of a teenage girl—white-blonde, tan, and lithe.

Elijah had materialized in the doorframe behind Jude and Annette. Her name came on a whisper from his lips. "Vivi?"

20

BEVERLY

Quinn arrived within forty-five minutes, looking spectacular. Almost uncomfortably so. Beverly became suddenly aware of her relative homeliness. Beverly had a natural drab look about her. Flat brown hair. Brown eyes. Washed-out skin. But she'd been trying. She'd been getting up each day and adding makeup, doing her hair, selecting accessories, and getting dressed like life went on.

And, mostly, life *had* gone on.

Still, Quinn put all of her efforts to shame. It was... inspiring, actually. Her fresh look magnetized Beverly to her, and Beverly wanted to know all of her secrets. Here was this woman, shrouded in peculiarity and unfamiliarity and living in a dump, and she breezed into the *Herald* looking like a movie star.

"Hi." Beverly smiled and waved Quinn over to her workspace—a tidy area just past the currently empty secretary's desk. "I'll introduce you to Forrest," she went on.

Quinn smiled nervously and shifted her handbag over. "Thanks again, Beverly," she whispered. "I appreciate this more than you know."

Beverly waved her off. "Oh, it's nothing. Like I said, you showed up in the nick of time. We really do need an update around here." Beverly walked her toward Forrest's office, where the door stood open.

She saw Forrest push up from his desk, his expression one of...*admiration*? Beverly couldn't be sure. She'd never seen it before.

"Forrest? This is Quinn."

He crossed the room and held out a hand. "Quinn," he said, his voice warm.

"Whittle. Quinn Whittle."

"Yes. Mrs. Whittle," he answered.

Quinn was quick to correct him. "*Miss.*"

Beverly smirked, but it quickly moved into a smile. She remembered the first time she met Tom. Creative Writing at the University of Michigan. She took it as a requirement for the journalism program. He took it as a requirement for his English teaching program. He was smart. She was shy. He was funnier. She was a better writer. They were assigned as critique partners. The rest was history.

Beverly swallowed and fell back a step. "I'll be out here if you need me," she said.

"Beverly, please," Forrest replied, "join us." He organized two chairs opposite his desk and the women sat. A sisterhood was fast forming, despite the fact that this was just their third or so meeting. Being neighbors sort of had that effect, maybe. Apple Hill was something of a sorority.

"Tell me a little about your background, *Miss* Whittle." Forrest lowered into his seat, his eyes never leaving Quinn.

Beverly looked at Quinn, too. Maybe she'd get a little more information about the notoriously private and peculiar new girl on the block.

"My background?" Quinn shifted in her seat, and her gaze slid to Beverly, who nodded.

"Sure. Previous work experience. Schooling? Volunteer work, even?" Forrest leaned forward, lacing his fingers together atop his desk.

"Right." Quinn settled back into her seat and set her jaw. "I was born and raised in Romeo. Went on to Wayne State and graduated with a degree in sociology. Minor in education." She swallowed and nodded. "Got married soon after. Had my daughter, Vivi. She's fifteen." A smile pricked the corners of Quinn's mouth. Beverly's own smile faded despite her best efforts, but Quinn quickly moved on. "After my divorce, I did some medical billing, receptionist work, and I spent a few years managing a tour company for Lake Huron. Down south," she added, clearing her throat.

"I bet your daughter loved that. She probably spent all her time on the water," Forrest commented. Beverly fidgeted. She'd rather not be there. She was ready to leave now. She had a story to write, after all. Something before she cracked into Carl Carlson.

Then again, maybe that's why Forrest wanted her here. Maybe they were both meant to dig into Quinn a little. See where the conversation went. Test her.

A stitch crinkled the skin between Quinn's eyebrows. "Yes. She...loves the water." Blinking rapidly, Quinn squirmed. Vivi was a touchy subject, obviously. Maybe Beverly need not be so sensitive about the daughter thing, after all.

"How does she feel about you two moving inland?" Beverly wondered aloud.

Quinn let out a breath. "Well, she's not moving inland." Her mouth fell into a line. "She lives with her dad."

21

QUINN

What Vivi had to do with Quinn's ability to make a Facebook post was beyond her. But she had no room to complain, so she rolled with it, being honest. Brutally so. It felt brutal, admitting that her own daughter didn't live with her. Like a perversion of nature. What mother didn't have custody of her child?

Quinn Whittle.

She saw surprise color Beverly's expression. And something *else* color Forrest's. Intrigue? *Relief?* She hoped not the latter. Because the whole reason Quinn was in Harbor Hills was to pull Vivi back to her. Not *win* her back. It wasn't a contest. Matt was a good dad. And Quinn knew she was a good mom. Two years ago, though, things had, well, fallen apart a bit. They had needed a change.

And now Quinn was ready to change back. She prayed every night that Vivi was, too. She prayed every night that Vivi would surprise her and call one day and say, *Mom, can I visit? Can I help you paint a bathroom? What's the best shop in your new town? Let's go!*

So far, though, their engagement had been limited.

"I don't know what it's like to have kids," Forrest added as filler. "Seems hard." He grinned, but Quinn noticed Beverly's face had assumed a vacant expression. Awkwardness pooled through the office.

"As for experience, I'm more than capable. A fast learner, for sure. I've used all basic computer programs and applications, and I've dipped my toes into social media." She nodded toward Beverly. "I understand that's the position. Social media manager?"

Forrest steepled his fingers together, and Quinn couldn't help but notice the bare left ring finger. She tried to concentrate on his face, but that, too, proved challenging. Gold-flecked green eyes sat across a broad nose. His Cupid's bow was lazy, dragging itself out longer over his top lip than was typical. It turned his mouth sensual, Quinn realized. Not a strong jaw. Curly, auburn hair, not yet graying at the edges or thinning on top. He was decidedly not the middle-aged man's man that his brother appeared to be. Dean Jericho looked every bit his name.

And, well, Forrest the Newspaper Editor was every bit his. Calm and reserved. A quiet strength, maybe.

Quinn wasn't sure about that yet. Not effeminate, but not overtly masculine.

Still, one thing was unarguable. Forrest Jericho oozed something that hollowed out Quinn's chest. Something that made her glad she got prettied up. Glad that she bought that nasty old house on Apple Hill Lane.

He cleared his throat and leaned back, crossing his arms over his chest. Muscles rippled along his forearms up to the edge of his cuffed shirt. "Social media, sure. Maybe some other work, too. If I'm being frank, I'd love to bring someone on board who knows marketing. Ads. SEO. Even website design."

Beverly scoffed. "That's a lot to ask for one position."

Forrest was clearly undeterred. "We're a small paper. We cut corners where we can, to be honest." He held Quinn's gaze, and she saw his Adam's apple bob at his throat. Desire—or something like it—churned within her, but she stamped it down *hard*. Quinn wasn't in the business of finding a lover. She wasn't the sort. Not even close.

And especially not when the man in question could potentially hire her. She was smarter than that.

"I don't have experience with any of that, to be equally honest, Mr. Jericho. But I'm smart, and I'm motivated. I'll do whatever you need me to." She wondered if she'd come to regret that line.

"I like your attitude," he answered, offering a grin, first to Quinn then to Beverly. "I think the next step is references."

Quinn gave a short nod and passed over a black leather portfolio. It was the same portfolio she had taken to every job interview she'd ever had. Not once had she been turned down for a position, and that meant the portfolio was a good luck charm, naturally. So, here it was. Inside were her résumé and three letters of reference. All former employers with glowing words. Just as Quinn had never been turned down for a position, neither had she ever been terminated.

Oh, no.

It was Quinn. She'd hit a wall. Something would happen—someone, a fellow worker, would transgress an invisible line. Perhaps they'd stroll out of the bathroom stall and skip past the sink. Or they'd make a remark—something so grating that Quinn would dwell on it and work it into a bigger deal than it ever should have been.

Or, sometimes, it was as simple as the monotony of it all. Whatever it was. Routines were fine—Quinn thrived with routines. But monotony was a whole different issue. Hours of mindless work. An idle brain was Quinn's most venomous enemy. No question. One would think she'd have found a career better suited to her nature. But then, the problem with that was that she'd come too far. Too far past college to return. Too far into a list of jobs to feel that she'd made a dent somewhere. And too far into the mess she'd made of her life to swim out.

Quinn Whittle was drowning.

She watched, her gut clenching, as Forrest reviewed the pages right before her eyes and Beverly's. It felt intimate, seeing him skim down niceties about Quinn. To see him read that she was the sort of worker they were sad to say goodbye to. Would he call these people, too? Right there in front of her? Would he ask Beverly what *she* thought? Right there, in front of her?

He shuffled the pages and then looked over top of them. His gaze fell on Quinn. "When can you start?"

22

ANNETTE

Annette blinked through the sunlight.

Jude had left her porch, striding tentatively down the steps and toward the idling truck with the two new faces. There sure were a lot of new faces on Apple Hill lately.

She glanced back at Elijah, whose jaw was still dangling open. Annette cleared her throat and glared at him. He came to and stepped up to the deck rail.

Annette watched Jude exchange inaudible words with the man and the girl. The man, at one point, pushed his hand through his hair. Exasperation. The girl, at one point, crossed her arms. Irritation.

This was not a happy visit.

Maybe it wasn't a planned one.

Annette bolstered herself and took off from the porch, joining Jude at the sidewalk.

"Hi," she butted in, although the trio had been silently studying the house next door upon Annette's approach. "Annette Best. You're Vivi." She smiled warmly and cocked her head to the girl.

The girl smiled back; hers was flat and put on, but this did not deter Annette Best. "You must be Quinn's daughter. Gorgeous like your mom." Annette winked, and the girl's face softened, but only just.

"Matt Fiorillo." The man stuck out his hand to Annette. He was handsome. About the same age as Quinn, which was close to the same age as Annette. Forties, probably. His last name was apparent in his dark hair and green eyes. The olive-colored skin matched his daughter's, something to set her apart from Quinn, whose complexion was a touch creamier. Days spent indoors, perhaps.

"I suspect you've come to see Quinn's progress," Annette pushed ahead, unsure what ground Jude had already covered. She dipped her chin to Jude as if to rustle up some conversational support.

Jude caught on, nodding. "Actually, it sounds like it's a bit more than that."

"More than a day trip?" Annette's smile broadened. "I just love dropping down to Birch Harbor for the day, myself. Sometimes my husband and son, oh—that's my son, Elijah." Annette boldly indicated Elijah up on the porch. She saw Vivi squint toward him then square her shoulders, narrow her gaze. Annette went on.

"Anyway, they rent a boat for the day and do guy stuff. Meanwhile, I stick to the little lakeside plaza."

"The marina," Vivi offered. Her tone was all ice. Know-it-all and sass, and Annette was ready for her.

"Marina, right. And a quaint one, too. Reminds me of the little dock by my parents' old house on Drummond Island. So precious." She smiled at Vivi, her eyes slits.

Matt cleared his throat. "Mrs. Carmichael says Quinn's out. Any idea when she'll return?"

"She's not answering her phone," Vivi complained, but Annette saw her steal another look up to the porch. She knew better than to follow the gaze. It'd humiliate Elijah. No, no. All she had to do was refer to him. That was more than enough to pique this little imp's interest. Her work here was done.

"She's at a job interview," Jude replied. "And, please, call me Jude."

Matt lifted an eyebrow beneath the hand he held to shield the sun. "Jude?"

Jude's face remained blank, and Annette realized these two knew each other. And things were…delicate, perhaps.

"She's been gone nearly an hour, I'd say. Should be back soon. You two are welcome to come in and have a glass of lemonade. Iced tea?" Annette waved back to her house, and Matt and Vivi exchanged a look.

"I think it's best they get in touch with Quinn right

away," Jude said carefully. She looked at Annette, a hardness filling her features. "Do you have the number for the *Herald*?"

23

JUDE

With her cell at home, Jude used Annette's landline, dialing the office of the newspaper and tucking herself down the hall as Matt and Vivi stood awkwardly in the kitchen.

Beverly answered on the third ring. "The *Herald*, this is Beverly Castle."

"Beverly, it's Jude, hi."

"Is everything all right?" Concern filled Beverly's voice.

Jude's response was measured as she leaned forward to glance toward Matt and Vivi. "We have a couple of people here who are hoping to see Quinn." It wouldn't do to alarm or excite anyone. Especially if Quinn was in the middle of an interview. "Beverly, I don't want to interrupt the interview. I just wanted to get an idea of when Quinn might be done. I hope that's okay."

"Well, sure. She and Forrest are just going over the hiring packet. She'll be finished soon. Maybe five minutes?"

"Will you be sure she heads straight home? Either that or maybe checks her phone?" Jude asked.

Beverly's voice dropped. "What's going on, Jude? Who's there?"

"It's—um...it's nothing. Everyone is *fine*. Like I said, just two visitors. Hoping to catch her. Can't get in touch is all. I don't really know Quinn, and I was worried maybe she didn't bring her phone with her. Maybe she'd run errands after, and"—Jude swallowed and glanced into the kitchen again before swiveling away—"I think these people are pretty anxious to see her. We've got them here in Annette's kitchen."

That did the trick. Beverly put the pieces together. Maybe she even figured who the special guests were. "I see. No problem. I'll mention that you called."

"But Beverly—"

"I'll be discreet. No sense in scaring her. Or scaring off my boss, either." A soft chuckle followed the latter comment, and Jude's body relaxed. Not only because Beverly assured her, but also because Beverly seemed...happy? Playful, even? Whatever it was, it was a good thing.

"Thanks, Beverly," Jude said earnestly before getting off the line and returning to the kitchen.

There, Annette was talking *at* Matt about the tedium of a small-town realty business. This sort of banter would bore the pants off the usual victim. But Jude saw something in Matt. Genuine interest? Appreciation, even? Whatever it was, Jude realized that Annette, though a bit of a gossip and possibly overmuch for most, was the right person for the job.

She also realized that Elijah and Vivi had wandered off.

Jude frowned, glancing through the foyer.

"Oh, Elijah took her to the backyard. I told him to." Annette smiled. "I know...I *know*." Then she smiled at Matt. "We've all been so excited to welcome another teenager on the street, that I was hoping Elijah could become Vivi's unofficial tour guide." She dropped her chin. "But I know. Vivi won't be staying. And that's just fine. It's not a bad thing to have friends in low places, as the saying goes." Annette threw her head back and cackled.

Matt seemed taken with her. In awe. Maybe even a bit of disgust. Jude couldn't help but laugh, too. Mainly at the circus act before her.

She tried to explain on Annette's behalf. "Harbor Hills would be the low place in her scenario," Jude said to Matt. "Anyway, how are things down south? The Hannigans? Kate?"

"Everyone is doing well. Very well," he answered. The words came out easily. Sincerely, and Jude knew them to be true. After a chaotic year for the family, it was a good thing that they'd all settled in.

She nodded. "I sometimes miss Birch Harbor. The smell of the Village. Your folks' restaurant. That *garlic* bread." She gave him a broad smile.

He returned it, but it faded quickly. "Have you been in touch with Gene?"

Jude's gaze slid away only to meet with Annette's raised eyebrow.

"Only as much as has been necessary," Jude replied, keeping her tone mild. "Annette, you and Matt have something in common, you know." A new subject was in order.

"Oh?" This intrigued the chatty Realtor.

"Did Matt mention he flips houses?"

Annette turned to him, her eyes wide. However, her response was the exact *opposite* of what Jude had hoped for. Annette pinned Matt with a searing stare. "No. No, he didn't. How convenient for *Quinn*."

24

BEVERLY

Once Quinn reappeared from Forrest's office, she beelined for Beverly.

"How'd it go?" Beverly asked her brightly.

Quinn grinned. "Great. I'm so thankful to you, Beverly. I think this will be a good fit. And I start tomorrow. I guess you're working on a story about Hills High? I have everything to get started from home, if I want. I don't have a computer set up yet, but—"

Beverly had yet to see Quinn so bubbly. It was a welcome change, and she hated to undermine that by shooing her back home, where who-knew-what was awaiting her.

"Do you have a computer? I can help you set it up today, if you'd like," Beverly offered, about to follow Quinn home just then to ensure she went straight there. "You can use your cell phone as a hotspot, if you have unlimited data. I do that when I'm working at a coffee house."

"Coffee sounds amazing," Beverly replied. "Are you free to take a break? My treat. As a thank-you. Truly, Beverly—"

"No. So sorry. I can't," Beverly cut her off.

"Sure, she can. We can all go for a celebratory drink, in fact," Forrest said behind them.

Beverly groaned inwardly and shot her editor a look, but he was a man. And he missed it entirely.

"A *drink*?" Quinn's eyes slid to Beverly, but Forrest was already jangling his keys in his pants pocket and tossing a file to a nearby desk.

"Coffee. Water. Whatever. The *Herald* is a social workplace. Casual. Right, Bev?"

Beverly winced. "Actually, I think Quinn wanted to get home and boot up her—"

"I'm game for a cup of joe." Quinn bit her lower lip, and Beverly worried she'd get her pale pink lipstick on her teeth. She did not. "I'd love to see a bit of the town, and I could use a couple of guides."

Beverly wanted to believe that Quinn was swept up in Forrest's charm, but something told her that wasn't it. That, instead, Quinn was lonely. She'd hate to be the one to rain on her emerging parade, but Jude had seemed to indicate that it was very important that Quinn go straight home.

There was nothing else Beverly could do. Her hands were tied. "Actually, Quinn, Jude called. Judith, our neighbor?"

Quinn's brow line crinkled. "For me?"

"I guess there's someone waiting for you?"

Forrest smirked. "Dean is needy for a handyman."

Both women looked at him in question.

"He shot me a text." Forrest shrugged. "Warned me you were coming. I already knew, but I guess something about you made my brother reach out ahead of your arrival." He gave her a winning smile. "It's a small town, Miss Whittle. Can't get far around here without someone exposing your secrets." Forrest winked at Quinn.

Quinn smirked. "If that's true, then I can see why you need to cut corners around here. The news circulates on its own, huh?" And then *she* winked at *him*.

As the three of them walked out of the white clapboard office on Main Street, Beverly explained that it wasn't Dean Jericho who was waiting for Quinn. Someone else.

Quinn froze on the front stoop. "Someone else?"

"I think so," Beverly confirmed.

"Who?"

Forrest took his cue and hung back, pretending to fiddle with the door.

Beverly lowered her voice. "I'm not sure. It seems important. I don't think Jude would have called otherwise."

Quinn seemed to understand. She glanced back at Forrest then at Beverly, apologetic. "It seems I do need to get back to my disaster zone. Can we raincheck for the coffee?"

Forrest joined them, his mouth in an easy smile and hands in his pockets, casual as could be. "Anytime. We can talk about how to best circulate the *news*," he added, one side of his mouth creeping up in a mischievous grin.

Forrest and Beverly watched as Quinn got in her car and waved from inside. They waved back, and Beverly turned to her boss. "I think she's going to fit in around here."

He nodded. "Are you sure you want to pursue her house for your new piece? Might scare her off."

"Off of the house or off of working for you?" Beverly asked. She liked the back-and-forth she had at the office. It kept her mind thrumming. These days, she needed a thrumming mind. Without it, she'd be in bed, a hot pad on her heart, and infomercials streaming across the television. A television she really wanted to toss. It was huge—Tom had liked oversized everything. It took up the whole of their bedroom wall, opposite the bed. She'd hated it while he was alive, always pointing out that he was a bed-reader, so why have a television in the bedroom at all?

Then, once he passed, she hated it for a different reason, of course.

Forrest took a step back to the office door. "How she handles your story depends on one thing."

"What do you mean?" she asked, following him inside, their would-be coffee break squashed by Quinn's leaving.

"On what you think happened to Carl Carlson."

"My angle?" Beverly answered smoothly.

He shook his head. "The truth."

25

QUINN

Quinn did not know who could have shown up at the house. No one who cared about her knew about her big move, save for Quinn's brother, who lived in Cleveland, and of course Matt and Vivi.

Matt and Vivi, however, were firmly planted in Birch Harbor for the remainder of the summer. And according to Vivi, she'd come visit when she *had time*. That meant when her local boyfriend had officially moved to Detroit, where he was starting college in the fall. So, by Quinn's estimation, she had at least a month until she could expect her daughter to appear.

Far likelier, Quinn would make regular trips down to the lake to visit them. Lunch at the Village or a play in the park—apparently there was a local drama troupe who put up productions each weekend. Not really Quinn's bag—and probably not Vivi's—but it could be something to share together. Then there was shopping. Maybe they could tour boutiques and antiques shops some Saturday morning. Vivi would love that—to play tour guide.

Again, however, all that depended on if Quinn could steal her away from the Indomitable Dominic, as Matt had started calling him.

Dominic Van Holt. The son of the mayor of Birch Harbor. Full ride to Wayne State. Potential out the wazoo. Likely to get into politics just like his father before him, but bigger politics. More influential circles. All that lay ahead of Vivi's very first so-called serious boyfriend.

The outlook for the pair was abysmal, particularly to Quinn. But Matt had egged Vivi on. He believed in high school sweethearts. In staying power. Despite the age difference. Despite modern young love.

Her mind returned to the mysterious guest awaiting her back on Apple Hill Lane. She turned into the neighborhood and took the first right.

Quinn scanned the strip of sidewalk, seeing the electrician's truck still there. The plumber's, too. And a third truck.

She frowned and searched beyond the windshield, but no one sat inside.

Quinn threw her car into park at the bottom of her

drive and tore out and up to her house, certain they were inside.

Certain this would *not* go well.

The place was still a dump, after all. Maybe if she'd been there to welcome them, she could have explained. She could have painted a picture. But cleaning up the mess in their heads after they'd already cracked into the place—it'd be impossible to reverse the imagery. No chance would they ever come back.

She arrived at the door, rubbing the pads of her fingers together compulsively, tapping out a pattern to soothe her nerves.

As she pushed open the front door, someone's voice called from down the street.

"Quinn!" It was Jude, standing in the space of no-man's grass between Quinn's property and Annette's. "They're over here."

A trapped breath slowly escaped through Quinn's puckered lips. She closed her eyes and pressed her hand to her chest before smiling at Jude and waving. "I'll be right over!" she called back.

Before she left her house, she checked briefly on Dean and the plumber. Both were knee-deep in Carl Carlson's ancient mess.

Dean told her he'd be another hour at least.

The plumber, however, asked Quinn to join him in the second-floor bath, where the rusty-bottomed clawfoot tub sat. That tub was a selling point for Quinn. She'd always wanted one. It was a bucket list thing for her.

She wished she could tell him she had something more urgent waiting at her neighbor's house, but he seemed distressed. Or at least as distressed as a crochety old plumber could be.

"What is it?" she asked, following him up the creaking staircase and around piles of Carlson leftovers.

"I wanted to test the tub before I moved on to the next thing," he answered, hoisting his jeans up to his belly button. His grubby fingernails scraped along a protruding belly, then he pointed to the tub as they stood in the doorway. "Clogged from here to Las Vegas." He chuckled, but his face fell into a scowl quickly.

Quinn blinked. "Okay. A clog?" Where could the guy be going with this? Even Quinn could have handled a clog. Gross, sure. But manageable.

"It's not the clog that I called you up for," he huffed and made a gargling sound in the back of his throat. "It's what I found when I cleared the pipe."

26

ANNETTE

Pursing her lips, Annette offered a refill to Matt. "More lemonade?"

He shook his head. "Thanks. Hope to be on my way after we connect with Quinn."

Annette glanced out the back door, trying to fill the uncomfortable silence that had fallen across the kitchen since Jude confirmed that she'd reached Quinn. "Now, where did Elijah wander off to?" She knew where, but Matt was getting bored with Annette's mindless chatter. Heck, *she* was getting bored with her mindless chatter.

The front screen door creaked on its hinges, and a set of footsteps followed. Annette scurried down the hall. "Jude! Quinn," she said, her voice lower on the second name. "We weren't sure what to do, really.

We're here for you. Whatever you need. You can talk with him in my kitchen...my bedroom...*wherever*." Annette gave her a serious nod, but Quinn seemed more excited than fearful.

"I don't care about *him*," she answered. "Where's Vivi?"

The three of them arrived in the kitchen, and Matt stood from a barstool, shoving his hands into his pockets. "Hey, Quinn."

"Hi, Matt." Nothing seemed to pass between them. As if they worked together, they were now totally unfazed and unimpressed one by the other. This surprised Annette, but then, she couldn't imagine divorcing Roman. If that ever happened, which it wouldn't, she'd pine after him for the rest of her days. Seeing her husband for the first time after an absence sent an electric jolt up her spine.

"Where is she?" Quinn cut to the chase, ignorant of Annette's and Jude's lingering. Ignorant of it or indifferent to it, perhaps.

"Uhh..." Matt glanced around, and Annette stepped forward.

"Elijah took her to the backyard to meet Sadie and show her his hideout." Annette snickered. "I know. A high school boy with a hideout. It's a fort he and Roman built when he was a kid. Now it's become something of a man cave for Elijah." She waved dismissively. "Anyway, Elijah's easy to get along with, you know. He's comfortable. Sweet. And he loves Sadie." Annette closed her mouth. She was blabbing again.

Quinn blinked. "Sadie?"

"Our lab. She lies on the back porch in a cool, shady spot. Though sometimes, she'll hang out in the fort. Or *man* cave." Annette bounced the heel of her hand off of her forehead and chuckled. "It's really—"

Quinn cut her off. "May I?" She gestured toward the back door and strode to it without waiting for a reply. Annette followed her, but Matt and Jude hung back together.

Beating her to the door with ease, Quinn pushed through it, her gauzy red blouse fluttering at her back.

Annette stayed at the door and gestured to her son. "Why don't you come in and help me with the dishes, E."

Quinn glanced back at her, her jaw set. No smile yet.

Elijah was smart and caught on quickly, excusing himself and joining his mom inside.

Annette lingered just one moment longer to see Vivi and Quinn fall into each other, a mess of white-blond hair and elegant, thin limbs. Swallowing her own emotion at the sight, Annette quietly closed the door and followed Elijah back in.

Matt smiled gratefully. "Mind if I wait in here?"

"Not at all," Annette answered. "Please, make yourself at home. Truly. On Apple Hill, we believe in the whole *mi casa es su casa* adage." She pursed her lips and pinned her hand to the table in recollection. "Gosh, Jude, do you remember—what? A year ago, maybe? It was like a revolving door the day before the Fourth. Everyone on the street was in and out of each other's houses, scrambling to help Jude pull off another great Freedom on Main event."

"I do." Jude smiled. "That was the first time since I've lived on Apple Hill that I had ever been in your house or Beverly's. Or Shamaine's." She giggled. "I thought Tom was going to kill me. I ran out of sugar for my sweet tea and popped in just as he dashed across the house half-naked from a shower. All that was between my eyes and his unmentionables was a white towel. I'll never forget the image. Burned into my brain." She laughed harder, and Annette joined in, too.

Elijah, disgusted or confused, meandered out of the kitchen and upstairs, retreating to his bedroom as he usually did.

Annette took a deep breath and let it out, the memory of the summer before sinking softly into her heart. "I actually went next door, to Carl's."

Jude cocked her head and frowned. "You did?"

After drawing a sip of her drink, Annette nodded. "Mhm."

Something shone in Jude's eyes. "So, you've been

there before, too, then? I mean before Quinn moved in?"

Annette shook her head. "Oh, no. He didn't answer." Then, something struck her. "Wait a minute, have *you*?"

27

JUDE

The back door opened, saving Jude from answering Annette's question.

"We're going to head over to the house. It turns out I was wrong after all." Quinn's smile was catching, and Jude immediately forgot about the exchange she had just had.

Jude looked at Vivi, whose expression undercut her mother's. Hidden behind a weak grin was a dash of pain. Something worrisome. Sad, even. "You're going to stay in town for a bit, Vivi?" Jude didn't know Vivi really, but she'd been around her enough in Birch Harbor to feel comfortable leaning in.

Vivi nodded. "Yeah." She cleared her throat and threw a furtive glance at her father. "For a bit."

"Viv, why don't you stay in here with the ladies. I'll walk your dad out. Be right back, okay?" Quinn brushed the backs of her fingers down her daughter's cheek affectionately, and Matt rose from the barstool. He crossed to his daughter and wrapped her in a bear hug, whispering into her ear. Jude thought she saw a lone tear escape down Vivi's cheek, but by the time Matt stepped back, it was gone. In its place, an icy stare.

A stare that Jude knew well. One she'd sometimes employed herself. Back before she'd made her big changes.

Quinn and Matt left, though not without a lingering look from Matt. Jude saw something in that look. Disappointment? *Disgust?*

Couldn't be. Were parents ever *disgusted* with their children? There was no way. Surely, there was no way.

Then again...Jude knew that, yes, actually, some parents could find their offspring...*disgusting.* She knew it all too well.

Empathy rose inside of her and she reached her hand out to Vivi, patting the girl awkwardly on the shoulder. "You're going to love Harbor Hills. It's like Birch Harbor without the constant threat of drowning." Annette, bless her heart, laughed for Jude.

Vivi did not. Instead, she glared. "Really? Because the moment we turned onto this street, I felt like I was."

"Like you were what?" Annette jumped in.

Vivi turned her gaze on Annette. "Drowning."

ONCE VIVI and Quinn had departed—without an explanation as to *why* Vivi was there so begrudgingly —Jude made her move to leave, too.

Before she stepped through the front door, though, she felt a presence looming behind her.

"I don't want to pry, really I don't," Annette said.

Jude turned back. "Pardon?"

Annette moved her hand to Jude's elbow, gripping it, sort of, in a polite way. A *warm* way. The pressure so light that it nearly tickled.

"The Carlson house. You've been *inside* of it?"

Jude felt the color drain from her face.

She hadn't done anything wrong, of course. But... did Annette really not *know*? It occurred to her that perhaps the Banks's' family history was more of a secret than she realized.

Now, here she stood, smackdab in the middle of a chance to keep it that way.

Considering her options, she figured there was nothing to hide. Not *really*.

But then if that were true, why did something deep down tell her to keep mum?

She worked her lips into a reply, a strangled sound slipping through. "Um, yeah. I think once. Just popped in with Christmas cookies one year. That was all."

"Wait, so—you *met* him?" Annette was flabbergasted, and she ought to be. No one had met Carl. No one had ever seen him. He was practically a ghost. Jude hadn't even met him, in truth.

Jude frowned. "No," she answered. "The door was left ajar. I just—um—I just popped it open, hollered a hello and set the cookies on a table by the door. In and out." She swallowed and let out a breath. "It was a mess. Wow."

Annette's nod of understanding came slowly, through a glazed-over expression. "Gosh, I don't think I have *ever* walked by and seen that door open." Then a grin curled on her lips. She lowered her voice. "If I did, though, you can bet I'd have peeked inside. But you"— her grin slipped away—"I can't see *you* doing that."

28

BEVERLY

Beverly emailed her latest article to Forrest and dragged herself into his doorway. "Sent," she said on an exhale.

He glanced up from his computer then looked back at the screen and navigated around, to his inbox, presumably.

Clearing his throat, Forrest read it aloud. He always did this. It was his process, as he called it. Caught quick errors before the article went for proof and press. Beverly cringed through the whole thing.

"Hills High Hires."

He smirked at her. "You know how I feel about alliteration."

She grinned back. "I couldn't help it."

Forrest read on.

"The end of the school year has seen not only the

commencement of seniors. So, too, have several faculty members left Hills High for new ventures.

"In total, the district reports that the lone secondary school of Harbor Hills Township has approved the retirement or resignation of nine critical employees. This number does not include three more employees who left for other reasons."

Forrest stopped and again looked up. "You sure you can cover this?"

Beverly swallowed and gave a short nod.

"Are you going to discuss Tom in this series?"

She shook her head. "No need. His leaving has nothing to do with the story. It's the story I'm covering."

Forrest didn't seem to accept this answer. He turned fully from his computer screen and laced his fingers on his desktop, fiddling his thumbs and staring at them before finally looking up again. When he did, a flat smile drew across his mouth. "Okay," he said, then read on, this time with a degree less enthusiasm and charm.

"Though the superintendent did not reply to a request for information ahead of printing, other sources were able to offer speculation as to the reason behind such a dramatic turnover in the space of one year.

"*Speculation*? We don't love that word, Bev," he chided.

She shrugged. "I'm trying to be decent."

"According to one such source, who prefers to remain unnamed, 'Hills High has lost its school spirit. Time to bring back a bit of the old school. If the school admin wants to keep good teachers, then it's time to do away with tests and bring back pep rallies. Like the old days!'"

Forrest didn't finish the rest. He bobbed his head from one shoulder to the other then stretched back in his chair. "It's a start," he offered.

"Well, it's the first in the series," she reasoned. "I'm warming up."

"You'll have to dig a little deeper."

"It's sensitive ground, Forrest," Beverly pointed out. "Typically, the local paper is supposed to celebrate its own high school. Not gossip about it."

"We're not gossiping. We're writing a series. A good story. Something to bring to light concerns and praise accomplishments. We can do both."

She nodded.

Forrest leaned forward. "Who are your sources, anyway? Are you"—he cleared his throat—"are you still in touch with your former contacts?"

Beverly couldn't help but smile at him. He was trying his best to use delicate language.

"The PTSO? Tom's colleagues?" She shook her head. "I'm not in touch with anyone."

He nodded. "What about Quinn? She has a teen daughter who'll be going to Hills High. Right?"

Hesitating, Beverly narrowed her eyes on the middle distance. "I'm not sure what her plans are for her daughter." Noncommittal was the way to go in such treacherous water.

"Talk to her."

"Aren't we saving her for a story on the Carlson house?"

"Ah, yes. The Apple Hill drama. Right. Yeah." He spun in his chair a full three hundred and sixty degrees. When he landed back facing her, he said, "Talk to Roman's wife. Best. Annie?"

"Annette."

"She's involved with the school, I'm sure."

Forrest wouldn't know who was involved in Hills High. They were only covering the piece because there wasn't much other news in town. But Harbor Hills being a family community, *everyone* wanted the scoop on the school.

"Another voice from Apple Hill. Why don't we reroute entirely and just do an exposé on the dramas of Crabtree Court?"

He grinned. "If you think it'll sell papers, then go for it."

"I'll talk to Annette."

Forrest nodded. "And I'll talk to Quinn."

29

QUINN

This was not how Quinn had hoped it would go.

Ideally, she'd have had the house nearly done by the time Vivi came around.

But Matt was adamant. Vivi needed a summer away.

Away from Birch Harbor.

Away from the lake.

And away from Dominic Van Holt, who was now no longer heading to Wayne State.

Quinn desperately wanted to ask Vivi to spill the beans. Instead, she had to focus on priming her daughter for the shock that would be stepping foot into her new summer getaway—696 Apple Hill Lane.

They stood together in the driveway, the last divide

between the normal, clean part of the street and the disaster zone that was Quinn's new house.

"You're not happy I'm here," Vivi complained.

Quinn's mouth fell open. She closed it and worked up an answer. "Are you *kidding* me?" She reached around Vivi's shoulders and pulled her daughter into her side, then kissed her head. Twice more.

"Mom, come *on*. Are you still doing that?"

Quinn feigned ignorance. "Doing what? And I'm *over the moon* that you're here. I'm just...well...I'm not ready. But that's okay," she rushed to add. "Maybe you'd be willing to *help* me? I could use a discerning eye."

"You want my advice?" Vivi crossed her arms and studied the house with a narrowed gaze. "Bulldoze the place and start over."

Quinn laughed. "Oh, come on. You haven't even seen the *inside* yet."

THE PLUMBER HAD FINISHED for the day—Quinn had stowed his discovery in the medicine cabinet for later tending. Now, all her attention was on her daughter, and there it would stay. Dean, the electrician, was still fiddling around. The plumber would return tomorrow to work the downstairs bath with a buddy. It was a two-man job, apparently.

Vivi's initial horror, upon walking into the foyer, had dissolved into subtle fascination. She'd even picked up a few of the Carlson leftovers, studying a piece of paper here, a tchotchke there. She asked questions on the tour.

How old was the house?

Over a hundred years.

When did the owner die?

Not sure.

Did he die in the house?

Don't think so.

Did he have a wife?

Don't know.

Is it haunted?

At that one, Quinn had belted out a laugh. "Yes. Haunted by the mess of ghosts past."

Vivi stopped mid-stair.

Quinn turned and rolled her eyes. "I'm joking. I've been sleeping here, and so far, no ghost. No bogeymen. Nothing more than junk."

"How long will it take you to get rid of all this? I mean...you've been here like a week. Longer, even, Mom. You could have emptied it first, right?"

"I'm working on it. You'll see."

And Vivi did. Once they made it to the second floor, Quinn showed her the progress. Both upstairs bedrooms had been emptied down to the stained baseboards and rotting flooring. Not so much as a speck of dust remained. Cleaned out entirely. Not scrubbed and sanitized quite yet, though. That would come when *everything* was out.

"Where are you sleeping?" Vivi asked as they veered into the bathroom.

"On the back porch."

"Where will I sleep? Maybe I should go back to Birch Harbor. I can stay with Clara."

Quinn's blood ran cold. "Well, I've been moving pretty slowly, I'll admit. Now that you're here, I'll go ahead and hire the cleaners for the upstairs. They can get working and have your room done in a day or two."

"Furniture?"

"We'll go shopping."

"So, what? I'll sleep outside with you until then?" Vivi's face broke. "Mom." Tears welled in her eyes, and Quinn's heart broke.

"Listen, listen, *shh*, Viv. Oh, Viv." She cradled her daughter's head. "Hey, come on. I've got an idea. I'll call the cleaners right *now*. I'll expedite *everything*. We'll get a room in a hotel in town. How about that?"

Quinn didn't exactly have the extra money for a hotel room. And she'd been waiting on hiring the cleaners until she'd made enough progress that she was able negotiate the price down. But she could pull from the savings. She could. She *would*. She had to.

Vivi lifted her head.

"Are there hotels here?"

Smiling, Quinn shrugged. No point in dishonesty at this juncture. "I guess we'll find out."

THE REST of the tour of the house didn't go half bad. The hope of enjoying a night or two in a hotel allowed Vivi to pretend to like the house—or at least see through the issues of it.

After seeing the electrician off and getting Vivi situated with her phone and bags in an old rocking chair on the front porch, Quinn withdrew her own phone. Thanks to the HOA meeting, she had half a dozen local phone numbers. It'd be best to start with those closest to her.

She had known Jude the longest, technically. But Beverly was now a coworker, and Beverly lived and worked in Harbor Hills full time. She'd have the best sense, probably.

Quinn found her contact and called.

Beverly answered after three rings, which Quinn took to be a good sign, naturally.

"Hey, Quinn! Everything okay?"

Her cheery voice was a departure, Quinn thought. Up to now, Beverly had come across a little morose. Brooding. Which made sense, of course. "Hi, Beverly. Yes! Well, kind of." She laughed nervously. "My, um, long story short, I have a—" Quinn flicked a glance through the front windows to Vivi. She wasn't embarrassed that Vivi was there. Of course not. She was embarrassed that Vivi wasn't *always* there. Questions were sure to follow, but Quinn wasn't ready for that yet. "I have a visitor who's looking for a hotel or some sort of accommodations in town. Do you know of a good place?" She winced before adding, "Preferably something...better than the current state of my house."

Beverly laughed, too. "Hey, now. Your house is about to be the best residence on Apple Hill. Just takes time. But yes. Of course. We don't have any hotels, if you're looking for a four-star experience. Or even three-star. There's the motel out on Harbor Boulevard, almost to Birch Harbor. That's a ways, though. We do have one place... Just off of Main Street. Bertie's. Bertie Gillespie. She runs a little B&B. It's adorable. A local favorite, for *sure*. I ran a piece on it a few years ago. Super quaint. Super charming."

"That sounds perfect." Quinn glowed. "Bertie's, then? On Main Street?"

"Bertie's on Main," Beverly confirmed. "There's a little wooden sign that reads Rooms to Let. Easy to miss—the sign that is. You'll see the house, though, if you look hard. Gorgeous green Victorian tucked behind a little grove of maples. Black iron fence that stretches along the sidewalk." Beverly chuckled. "Sorry. Talking about Bertie's sort of transports me to my article."

Quinn smiled. "It sounds lovely. Your writing, I mean. And Bertie's." She let out the breath she'd been holding. "Okay, Bertie's on Main Street. Green Victorian. Maples. Rooms to Let."

"I can meet you there. I'm just down the way. Still at the office, wrapping up a project," Beverly said.

Hesitating, Quinn realized this was the moment of truth. Beverly would meet Vivi. Quinn would have to come clean. Maybe Beverly would be uncomfortable, even. Vivi, too.

"I'm sure we can find it," Quinn replied.

"I bet I could get you a good deal," Beverly answered, dangling a succulent carrot over the phone.

"Really?" The hope in Quinn's voice bordered on pathetic. Desperate. Oh well.

"Bertie just so happens to be my mom."

30

ANNETTE

After Jude left, Annette was satisfied. Satisfied that her mysterious, newly divorced neighbor was a little more interesting than she had realized.

With the height of the sales season in full swing, she should be at the office, wishing business into existence. So, that's exactly where she went.

Best on the Block offices were located on Main Street, along with every other business in Harbor Hills. Though it was far short of an industrial district, one could find just about everything on Main. Their office was a brick square nestled snugly between Harriet's Hardware and Dr. O's, the local veterinarian. The monthly rent was more than either Roman or Annette wanted to pay, but they both figured that the prime real estate, so to speak, was a necessary evil.

"Honey, I'm home!" Annette called out as she stepped in through the wood door. Their welcome chimes clinked above her head, and she hung her purse on the hat stand. Roman always said she'd better not do that—liable to get ripped off. But the office was a one-room box with three-hundred-sixty visibility, save for the bathroom at the back. There was no way she'd miss a pickpocket or burglar, and their particular row was secured with an alarm, thanks to the landlord.

Roman looked up at her above his rimless readers. Annette couldn't believe she was married to someone who wore readers. But there he was, looking dashing and salt-and-pepper-haired and...entirely deflated.

"What's wrong?" she asked, joining him at his desk. Ropes of numbers bled across his computer screen, and Annette felt a headache prick to life behind her eyes.

He massaged his temples and tried for a smile. "Just...running through some figures."

Annette frowned at the screen, pretending to make sense of it all. Then she gave a flourish of her hand. "Any leads today? New clients? New listings? Old listings with new prices? Haven't peeked at my report yet."

"No price changes on our current listings. I talked to the Mainards. They want to hold firm at two-fifty. I heard from the Becketts. They aren't willing to settle for *another* three-bedroom. Definitely want four. Definitely need more space."

Annette's lips drew down. "What's wrong with a three-bedroom?" The Becketts were a Crabtree couple. Younger. The wife was expecting, and they already had one child. The little two-bedroom on Dogwood was about to be too small. Even Annette could admit that. But on their budget—he was a teacher, she a stay-at-home mom—they'd be lucky to find anything at all.

"I told them if they'd wanted four, they should have taken the Carlson foreclosure," Roman said.

Annette replied, "But she's pregnant. That place is way too much work."

"Well, we have no other four-bedrooms in their price range," Roman reasoned.

"Why four? Why not three?" Annette knew she was arguing unnecessarily. Roman wasn't her client. The Becketts were.

"Didn't you hear?" he asked, pulling his glasses all the way off and leaning far back in his office chair. It squeaked. Loudly.

"Hear what?"

"Twins." He smirked. "They want more space than three bedrooms. I guess Elora is going to find a work-from-home job after she delivers."

"Twins!" Annette clasped her hands, skipping over the second bit of news. "Twins! Harbor Hills has *no* twins. Oh, wow. I'm...I'm totally jealous."

Roman chuckled. "You and everyone else. Those

two kids are going to be town royalty. They're already famous. Can't believe you didn't know."

"I've been distracted," Annette said. "Anyway, what will she do? Sell Mary Kay?"

"Who knows? I just got the email this morning. Twins. Four-bedroom *for sure*. One room can be a home office or a den."

"Oh! Well, three-bed-plus-den is different than four bedrooms. Don't we have a listing like that? North of town?"

Roman shook his head. "Nope. And anyway, they're not likely to get enough for their house to help upgrade, twins or no twins."

Annette nodded. "Right." Then, she thought for a moment. "Speaking of local kids, did you hear? Quinn's daughter is in town now."

"Quinn?" Roman's brow line furrowed.

She rolled her eyes at him. "*Quinn*. Our new neighbor?"

"Right, right." Roman pushed his glasses back on and returned to his screen. "Well, that's nice. New friend for Elijah. Ever since Kayla—"

Annette saw his jaw tense as the name fell out of his mouth and drifted away. Her chest seized. Elijah had loved Kayla. Not like *that*. But he'd loved her since they were kids. They'd grown up together. In truth, Kayla's death had wedged something between Annette and Beverly. Between Elijah and Beverly, actually. And the wedge was catching, turning the whole Best family on Beverly, ultimately. Only recently had feelings between the two thawed. The pain. The blame. Always self-inflicted, no matter who bore it.

"Maybe," Annette whispered. "Although, I'm not sure she'll be staying."

Roman, distracted once again by his spreadsheet, looked up, his eyebrow cocked. "Not staying? What do you mean? Quinn's leaving?"

"No, not Quinn. Quinn is staying, as far as I can tell. Vivi, though. I think she'll be going home. To Birch Harbor. At least eventually. That's the impression her father gave me when he dropped her off."

"Her father? Birch Harbor?" Roman pushed his chair away from the desk and gave his wife a serious look. "How involved are *you* in this mess?"

"Oh, Roman," Annette tsked. "It's not a *mess*. It's a family. They are...oh, I don't know. They're finding their way!" She threw up her hands. "It's Apple Hill. Is anything ever perfect on Apple Hill?"

He gave her another look. "It used to be."

31

QUINN

Trusting a stranger—even if Beverly wasn't all that strange to Quinn—felt a bit like a freefall. What if Bertie's was no better than the run-down motel on the outskirts of town? What if it was way, *way* better than a run-down motel? And far out of Quinn's price range? Even with the "friends and family discount" Beverly hinted at?

After packing an overnight bag and shuffling Vivi and her suitcase to the car, they made off, out of Crabtree Court and down Ruthenberg Avenue toward Main Street.

The town reminded Quinn quite a lot of her childhood. The single, narrow thoroughfare was lined in angled slots for parking, but few were taken.

Both sides of the two-lane street were lined with storefronts and businesses, carved out of old residences, every last one. One particular strip looked like an old rowhouse, and Quinn spied Best on the Block, the letters blurring in her vision as she refocused ahead.

A little sidewalk sale was in full swing on the opposite side. Three shops in a string had put out signs touting deep discounts and fresh lemonade.

Quinn's gaze slid to Vivi. "Should we stop and browse?"

Vivi had been spying the small-town spectacle, too. She looked back at her mom, her mouth in a firm line. "Let's get to the hotel first. Maybe we can walk back."

It was generous, Vivi's offer. So generous that a deep well of gratitude rose up in Quinn's chest. She smiled broadly. So broadly her cheeks nearly squeezed tears out of her eyes. Not quite, though.

At the end of the parallel strips of homes-turned-public-locales, the street-side parking spots disappeared beneath shady trees.

Then, just beyond the change from business to private life, Quinn spied it. A green Victorian, tucked back. It was the green she saw, somehow, despite how it blended so well with the trees. Not the sign, though her eyes flicked about the front of the property until they found it.

Rooms to Let.

A woman popped out of a parallel-parked car and

waved to them. Beverly. Bertie's daughter and now Quinn's neighbor.

Quinn figured in her head. Beverly Castle. Formerly Beverly Gillespie. Harbor Hills local. Now a widow and—what was it you called someone who lost a child? Like...a reverse orphan. A tragedy.

But now, waving back at Beverly through her windshield, she didn't see the downtrodden woman that Beverly was. She saw a happy, even *excited* forty-something. Warm brunette hair bouncing on her shoulders. Blue bangles like elegant shackles sliding down her arm as she finally lowered her hand from its wave.

"Here we go," Quinn said on an exhale.

She parked, barely, in the spot behind Beverly. Vivi waited until Quinn had alighted onto the sidewalk before she opened her door and joined them.

Beverly smiled and gestured back through the maple grove. "This is it. Bertie's. Kind of a secret gem."

"It's beautiful." Quinn beamed. And it was. Just as Beverly had described it. Quinn imagined Beverly was good at her job. A staple to the *Herald*. No wonder she was so comfortable with Forrest. He probably saw her as the crux to his operation. Quinn could never imagine being important to someone like Beverly probably was.

The moment Forrest came to mind, Quinn felt a rush of...*something*. Butterflies? Couldn't be. The last time she'd felt butterflies over a guy was Matt. And that was fifteen years ago.

Quinn and Vivi followed Beverly through the maple trees and up a set of crumbling concrete steps. The disrepair reminded Quinn briefly of her own hovel, but she pushed on until the trio swung through the door and into a narrow, charming reception area. Ebony wood mixed with light oak mixed with porcelain flourishes, and the whole of it came together, somehow. That was the essence of Victorian, perhaps. A touch hodgepodge, but not enough to be off-putting. Just enough to look a bit like a gingerbread house, perhaps. Quinn wondered if she'd go this route in her décor, but just as quickly decided against it. She didn't have the money, for starters. No. She'd be full-on hodgepodge, probably. Pulling pieces from yard sales and consignment shops and big-box stores with particle board shelves. Shuddering, Quinn hoped the job at the *Herald* turned into something. She really, *really* did.

"Beverly!" a black-haired woman sang from behind the broad check-in desk. She rounded it and, as she neared, Quinn saw that she looked nothing as she'd have expected Beverly's mother to look. The black hair was dyed and a touch too black, if that was possible. She'd drawn on eyebrows, a centimeter too high over her eyes and, again, midnight black. Her green eyes pierced through all the false color and thickly coated lashes, clashing with heavy circles of rouge—one on each cheek. A black blouse and black bangles offset the white pants the woman wore. Despite all the garishness, Quinn felt a magnetic pull to the woman. Much like her little inn, there on Main Street, she...*came together*, somehow.

"Mom," Beverly pretend-moaned, a genuine smile creeping up her cheeks as she braced herself for a two-cheek kiss from the woman. Quinn wondered if this woman was the one thing keeping Beverly going. Maybe Bertie of the Bed-and-Breakfast was *it*. Another important someone.

Quinn withheld her sigh and tried for her own sincere smile. It came easily. "You're Bertie, I suppose?" She fingered the buttons on her blouse, counting silently to three, three times.

"That's my name, and don't wear it out." She tossed her head back, cackled, and blindly grabbed for Quinn's hand, shaking it at first then tugging her in for a hug. "And you're Quinn. Our new girl in town. And who might *this* model be?" Bertie raised her waxy arches as she looked Vivi up and down with the drama of a theater director.

Quinn watched as Vivi preened under the inspection. She handled herself well enough that Quinn need not make an introduction.

"I'm Viviana Fiorillo," Vivi replied. "From Birch Harbor, though not originally."

Bertie's eyes widened and she stole a glance at Quinn. "Well, that still leaves me searching. Sisters? *Twins?*" She winked at Quinn who suppressed an inward groan.

"Vivi is my daughter, but that compliment will *never* get old," she said as casually as possible. To her surprise, though, Vivi took it in stride.

"I look nothing like my dad. Other than my skin tone." A little smirk drew across her mouth, and Quinn stilled herself for a snub, but it never came. Instead, Vivi said, "Everyone says I look like my mom." She shrugged, and her mouth pricked up in a lopsided smile. "I happen to agree."

32

JUDE

J ude had promised Annette that she'd arrive the next morning to help at Quinn's. However, there were two problems.

One, that Quinn hadn't given them the green light to help.

Two, Jude had an interview. That afternoon. With the principal of Hills High for a particular English opening that the school had yet to fill. This could be awkward.

Assuming Beverly rolled around at some point.

Then again, she shouldn't. She worked during the days. Just like Annette was supposed to. That was the silver lining to having a slow business, perhaps. Annette could fill her free time with charitable acts and still end the day on a high note.

Jude envied her strong will.

"Good morning!" Annette trilled as Jude stood on her doorstep, a big plastic tub in her arms. She'd filled it with her most portable essentials. A box of baking soda, a bottle of vinegar, rags, SOS pads, a scouring brush, and more. Annette propped her hands on her waist. "Well, aren't you prepared?"

Elijah appeared behind his mother, wearing something far too nice to be deemed work clothes. Jude felt a little insecure about her own paint-stained shirt and overalls.

Then she remembered that Vivi would be next door, and his hip band T-shirt and just-ragged-enough jeans made sense.

Jude greeted them both then jutted her chin toward Quinn's. "Any chance you've heard from her? I only have a couple of hours to spare."

"In fact, yes. She's—hesitant. But with the deadline of the block party coming up, I think she feels as desperate as we do."

Jude wasn't especially desperate. It didn't matter to her if locals visited Apple Hill Lane and their first impression happened to be a fixer-upper. That certainly mattered to Annette, however. Jude understood this even more clearly since the Bests had put their own house on the market.

Annette and Elijah left for a moment and returned with some supplies in hand. Elijah with a box of heavy-duty black garbage bags and Annette with a mop bucket, mop, and a bottle of Simple Green peeking out.

They lined up and marched down Annette's front walk and over to Quinn's. Gone were the electrician's truck and the plumber's, which meant Quinn would be alone inside with Vivi. Jude could just picture it. They'd be bickering. Tired from a night in a motel, even if it was the adorable little inn on Main Street. Jude had spent one or two nights there over the years. It was a landmark, after all. Bertie's. Bertie's B&B. Too cute for words, really. Jude would love to do something like that. Run a motel or an inn. It sounded like something out of her favorite books—those women who got a divorce, then stumbled into a windfall and resurrected a desperate, deteriorating old place and restored it to something quaint and charming and all those words that had become so trendy of late.

Then she remembered the job at hand.

Annette's fist shot out to the door and gave it three sharp raps.

Elijah sulked behind them. He was both glad to be there and embarrassed, it would seem. And the glad part was only apparent by the fact that he'd come at all. Most teen boys wouldn't be caught dead hauling trash out of a neighbor's house, especially when the neighbor happened to have a pretty daughter.

Elijah wasn't like most boys, apparently.

The door opened, sucking with it some of the heat

from the porch. But as Quinn ushered them inside, Jude realized there was no air conditioning in the house. Just a few fans, stationed to move hot air out and drag cool air from...somewhere.

It was the twenty-first century. How had Carl Carlson not at least installed window AC units?

Jude kept her surprise to herself and took the place in.

It was wholly unfamiliar. Hard to believe Jude lived on the same street as 696.

"It's rough, I know," Quinn confessed, possibly catching Jude's frown.

She shook her head. "Oh, no. That's not what I was thinking at all." She looked around meaningfully. "You've made excellent progress—it looks like. And this place...it's going to be a beautiful home. I know it will." She smiled, and Quinn just gestured them to the kitchen.

Vivi was nowhere to be seen. Quinn had the antiquated fridge and freezer doors propped open, and a rag hung over the top door.

"Are you keeping that?" Jude neared the old appliance, marveling at its condition. "This must be over fifty years old!"

Quinn shrugged. "I don't have much choice. The electrician and plumber blew through half my budget. Almost."

The admission felt intimate. Jude was unused to

talking finances with anyone. Even with Gene, they'd kept things separate. Each month, she'd cut him a check for her half of the mortgage, utilities, groceries, and anything else that made up a life. At the start of their marriage, he'd described the plan as the best way to *share*, even though it had distinctly rubbed her wrong. By the end, she realized it was his way of keeping them separate. All along, they'd been separated. All along.

"Oh, no," Jude answered. "I am not passing judgment. Well—I *am*. In a good way." She laughed nervously but quickly rounded back to her original sentiment. "This thing is gorgeous. I can't believe how beautiful it looks after so many years. And so many...*owners*."

Annette swung her head into Jude's view, her interest obviously piquing at any indication that Jude knew more than Annette did about the goings-on of Apple Hill.

Annette said, "I went through the history of ownership. Not many folks have lived here over the years."

Surprised lifted Jude's eyebrows. "You did?"

Annette nodded. "Sure, I did. Once the bank reached out with a request for help, I dove right into it. Carl moved in sometime in the nineties. Before we were here. And before you," she added for Jude's benefit. "But before *Carl*, it belonged to his own family, in fact. Other Carlsons."

"So, his name wasn't fake?" The voice came from the doorway at the back of the kitchen. Vivi. Her stare was cloying. Her outfit, too. A white tank top that hardly hit her navel. Cut-off jean shorts that were cuffed at the thigh. Long tan legs stretched down into white Keds. Absent was a paint-stained T-shirt for cleaning a house.

Annette hesitated just briefly before answering. "Not his *last* name, at least. Carlson. Long line of them. They were early founders of the area, I guess." She shrugged then looked at her son. "Do they teach local history at Hills High?"

He tore his gaze from Vivi and fumbled through a reply to his mother. "Local history?" he asked.

"Right. Do you learn about local history? Is Carlson a big name?" Annette pressed her hand against her chest, looking to Jude then Quinn. "I'm not *from* here originally. I was born on Drummond Island. Grew up there. Small towns are my thing, but we only moved here to be closer to Roman's parents."

His mother's question lost in her banter, Elijah had turned bored-looking.

"Quinn," Jude said, cutting to the chase. She had only a bit of time, after all, what with her interview coming up. "Tell us where to start."

Quinn smiled at Jude, and her shoulders fell down as though she were releasing a hundred years of pent-up anxiety. Then, she rolled them in circles three times through before cranking her head to each shoulder in a quick stretch. "I'm to the point now where all I want to do is to get rid of *everything*. And frankly? I don't care how that happens."

"So, yard sale? Are you free on Saturday? We could probably organize one. Keep things easy. No running out to find places willing to accept donations," Annette prattled.

"St. Vincent de Paul will come by and pick up anything worthy of donation," Jude pointed out. "You can have the best of both words. A little spare cash *and* you can unload some of the items that don't sell, sending them off to a good cause."

"Let's do it," Quinn said, propping both hands on her hips. "Yard sale. Move everything that isn't an appliance or major piece of furniture to the driveway. Is rain in the forecast before Saturday? I saw some tarps in the garage."

"I have one in my, um, fort," Elijah offered a little shyly.

Quinn smiled gratefully at him.

"What if we find something that looks, I don't know, *super* valuable?" Vivi asked, her eyes narrowed on her phone.

"Did you find something super valuable?" Quinn replied in kind, cocking her head.

Vivi's head shot up. "No," she answered, rolling her eyes. "But if we do. I mean look at this place. It's just a matter of time before we stumble across hidden cash or...or some big, dark secret."

"If you find something valuable," Jude cut in, "bring it to me." And then, for good measure, she winked.

33

BEVERLY

Beverly made her way to Hills High to interview Darry Ruthenberg, the high school principal, regarding the turnover. Quinn and the history behind 696 Apple Hill would have to wait. It'd make for a better October series, anyway.

Right now, Beverly needed to dig deep and make something for her current story. This piece would go beyond reporting the news. It needed to become a human-interest feature. Why were teachers leaving the school and what was the school doing about it?

The drive was only a few miles long—from the newspaper office on Main to the school, which sat at the very end of Schoolhouse Street, an obvious name for the street upon which Harbor Hills' very first one-room schoolhouse was built.

Hills High was developed out of that single-room building, added on and around until it was a towering school building that comfortably housed up to a thousand schoolchildren. Mind you, Hills High had never in its history matriculated even half that many schoolchildren. Though the roaring twenties were a promising time for the small town, nothing materialized in the way of big industries. No motor vehicle factories. No tourism draws. And years on, still nothing came to town that would draw more families.

Beverly sometimes wondered why she had convinced Tom to come back here to begin with. And she wondered what might have happened if she hadn't.

Being back at the school felt like a test. A cruel test. The last time Beverly was on campus would have been for parent-teacher conferences in the fall of the year before. She'd hated parent-teacher conferences. She ought to have looked forward to them. Kayla was a good student. A *great* student. And she was a good girl, too. Her teachers loved her. Classmates, too. And this wasn't just a post-mortem declaration of the goodness Beverly had wished she'd seen in her daughter. It was the truth.

Still, Beverly always worried that she'd arrive at a conference and be blindsided. That Kayla had hidden something from her. And there were no grounds for this. Nothing that precipitated such dread. It was just, plainly, Beverly's own bottled-up fears or guilt, though about *what*, she didn't know.

Sitting there, in the parking lot, she tried to see things about the school she'd never seen before. Things distinctly separate from the student body. Things that could fill out her story and pacify Forrest, whom Beverly decided was evil for sending her on this mission.

Then again, the story was *Beverly's* idea.

She'd been blocked for so long. It started before the accident, actually. At least six months before. After fifteen years of writing good stories for the *Herald*, she'd begun to wonder if her time was up. If she was out of juice. Burned out.

Now she was here, at one of *those* places. The places she connected acutely with Kayla.

Maybe that's *why* she had picked Hills High for a story.

Maybe Beverly would find Kayla there, like she'd been locked up in after-school detention this whole time. Maybe it was there, at the school, where Beverly could wake up from her nightmare.

HALF AN HOUR LATER—AFTER compiling the energy and strength to leave her car and enter the building— Beverly found herself sitting in a blue plastic chair across from a nosey secretary who kept stealing glances over her computer screen.

Finally, after the third glance, Beverly withdrew her tape recorder and notebook and laid them across her lap. She smiled at the woman, who now stared plainly.

"So," Beverly narrowed her eyes on the nameplate on the desk, and a memory shot up her spine and into her head.

The first day of Kayla's freshman year, Beverly brought her. Tom was in his classroom, tending to his promise that he wouldn't tell anyone that he was Kayla Castle's dad, despite the obviousness of the fact—small town and same last name.

They shuffled in on an autumn breeze, among a throng of other first-day students. Kayla already had her schedule, but Beverly knew the staff at Hills High. She'd been to any number of faculty Christmas parties and had even hosted one or two of her own. She wanted to say hi and introduce her beautiful daughter, now a teenager, to all those people who had previously known Kayla as just a girl. It was a point of pride, Beverly's joining Kayla on the first day, beginning with the old secretary and striding casually through the front offices, borderline boastfully.

This secretary, though, was unfamiliar. Not the same one from that first day of school. The one Beverly had known. The one who'd come to the funeral.

This was a new one.

Maybe that wasn't so bad.

"Miss Elaine?"

The woman's smile lit up. "Elaine, yes. Hi." She beamed. Beverly wondered if it was the thrill of meeting a local celebrity widow or something else. The woman answered the unspoken question quickly. "I've never met a newspaper reporter," she gushed. "I feel so...*important*."

"Well, I'm mainly hoping to speak with Principal Ruthenberg." Darry Ruthenberg, another Harbor Hills descendant. Just like Beverly. More prominent, however, because a local street was named for his ancestors. Unlike Beverly's maiden name, which was relegated to bits of old-time scandal and new-age familiarity.

"Oh, yes. He'll be out very shortly. I know he will. He's just finishing an interview for a new English teacher." Elaine's smile didn't fade. Her lips never twitched. She really was new. The only thing she seemed to know about Beverly was her job.

Not her past.

Beverly smiled back. "Right. That's sort of why I'm here."

Elaine's eyebrows rose. A glimpse of small-town gossip mere inches away from her grasp. They quickly fell, though, into a jagged line of confusion above her heavily lined eyes. "Wait a minute. You're here to *interview*?"

Beverly chuckled. "No. I'm here to find out about the turnover. Get a little glimpse into the life of a small-town school administrator. The challenges. I hope to draw positive attention to the school, first and foremost. But also, I think people want to have a behind-the-scenes look into Hills High. It's, in many ways, the cornerstone of our community."

Just then, the door behind Elaine swung open.

Instead of Darry Ruthenberg, however, a different familiar face appeared.

"Jude?" Beverly's eyes grew wide.

Jude returned the stare. "Beverly. Are you—"

"Beverly?" Darry Ruthenberg made his way around Jude and joined in the confusion.

Elaine took her cue, too. "Mr. Ruthenberg, Miss Castle is here with the *paper*, you see. And Mrs. Banks is here to interview, and well—it would appear you all know each other and so—"

Beverly smiled at Darry, and—to her surprise—it came easily. Warm and soft and filled with far-back memories. Not near ones.

"Beverly?" Darry repeated, as if he was confused that she was there. As if he wasn't expecting her.

But, of course, he was.

She swallowed. "Hi, Darry." Blinking, her gaze

danced back to Jude. "Well? Is Jude going to be Hills High's next English teacher?"

"That depends," he answered and slipped his hands into his pockets. A shy smile curled up his cheeks, and he dipped his chin toward Jude, "on whether *Ms.* Banks accepts the position."

Jude pursed her lips, but she quickly allowed a broad smile to lift her face. "I do."

By suppertime, they'd made terrific progress on cleaning the house.

Vivi had found a new energy, too. Impressing the sweet neighbor boy with her out-of-town exoticism and quick wit had brought her out of her coolness.

After Annette and Elijah had left—and long after Jude had gone—the mother and daughter folded themselves into Quinn's car to drive up to Bertie's for another night.

Once on the road, Quinn could not help but pry. "So, Viv. What happened?"

"What do you mean? Upstairs? Well, I found a little charm or something—" She started to dig into her jeans pocket, but that wasn't Quinn's question.

"No. Not at the house. I mean at..." Her mouth

turned dry over the word *home*. There was no way she could use it. Not if she was trying to wage a campaign to bring Vivi to Harbor Hills more permanently. At least part time. At the *very* least part time. "I mean back in Birch Harbor."

"Dad told you," Vivi snapped, giving up on finding the charm and crossing her arms over her chest.

"Actually, he didn't." Quinn added, "Not everything, at least."

Vivi threw her a sidelong glance. "He told you I was in trouble."

Raising an eyebrow, Quinn kept her focus on the road. "He said there had *been* some trouble. Not that you were *in* trouble."

"Same difference," the girl huffed and turned her head to the window. "Everything was fine. No—it was *great*. Then Dominic had to go and lose his scholarship."

"How?"

Vivi let out a sigh. "It's a long story."

"I've got time."

"We're almost to Bertie's." The way Vivi said it— *Bertie's*, like it was a grandmother's name, or an aunt's. Like Harbor Hills was already ingrained in her. So soon. So easily. Quinn savored this moment. Maybe this town, though not their own, could become part of them together. They could be new there together, and a piece of this new place could be theirs—something to share. Mother and daughter.

"Well," Quinn said, pulling into a spot outside the inn, "when you want to talk about it, I'm here."

Vivi didn't budge. She didn't move to unbuckle her seat belt. She didn't reach beneath her thigh to scroll through her phone compulsively. Instead, she turned to her mother. "He cheated."

THEY WERE each tucked in their own beds, the room dark and small around them.

Quinn asked simply, quietly, "*Cheated?*" The word alone was enough to conjure back up the conversation they'd left at Bertie's front door.

"Not on *me*."

Now, she was confused. "Okay, so, you said Dominic *cheated*. But not on you?"

"Right," Vivi confirmed. Her voice was clear, and it was all Quinn had to focus on in the blackness.

Quinn's breath hitched. Was this the moment? The last time Vivi had lived with her—two years ago—they'd had *the* conversation. The birds and the bees. The whole thing proved to be even more awkward than Quinn could have predicted, particularly once Vivi shot her down with a quick and flat, "*I already know.*"

Quinn hated that her daughter *already knew*. Now, here they were. Potentially on the brink of the second phase of that conversation. More birds. More bees. And now a villainous boyfriend added to the mix. "Were you two"—Quinn swallowed past the lump, crafting her phrasing carefully—"*serious*?"

Vivi's reply came fast. "What? Ew, *Mom*! No! This isn't about *that*."

Quinn's chest deflated and she shifted on her pillow to get more comfortable. A *whew* silently escaped her lips, then she said, "Oh, right."

A quiet beat spanned across the distance of the twin beds. Yes, twin. Bertie's was old-fashioned to a fault. Quinn didn't mind, though.

"It was the SAT," Vivi whispered.

"What was the SAT?" Quinn whispered back, matching her daughter's conspiratorial tone.

"That he cheated on."

"Dominic cheated on the *SAT*?" Quinn felt...unimpressed. To say the least.

"Mhm. And they caught him, and he lost his scholarship. So, that's why he's staying in Birch Harbor instead of going to Detroit."

"But not why *you're* here in Harbor Hills," Quinn pointed out gently.

Vivi shifted in her bed loudly, tossing sheets, tugging them, maybe. Quinn couldn't see her to know, and the sounds seemed put on.

"Dad *told* you," she huffed.

"He didn't. I promise, Viv." Quinn blinked in the blackness. Then again. One last time.

"They think I'm the one he cheated *with*."

"What? That makes no sense."

"He snuck his phone into the testing room, and he texted...*someone*."

The tug of exhaustion coupled with the exhilaration of Vivi's unprecedented bonding had Quinn feeling dizzy in her bed. Confusion colored her thoughts as she made some sort of meaning from Vivi's explanation. "Okay," she said, shifting to face Vivi in the darkness. "You're saying Dominic took his phone into the SAT test—which isn't allowed—then texted someone for, what? Answers? Who did he text?"

Her daughter made a sound of exasperation. "I mean—some *girl*."

"I'm sorry, Viv. I'm tired, and I'm not following."

"*Mom*, all that matters is that he cheated on the SAT and got caught."

This was still weird. "But you had nothing to do with it," she said flatly.

"I positively did not help him cheat on the SAT."

"Okay, then. Do you think he *was* cheating on you? With this...accomplice?"

"Mom, *no*." Vivi was losing her patience fast. Quinn had to get her act together.

"Okay, well, whatever happened—it's not *your*

fault. It's Dominic's. Right?" Sleep was pulling hard at her brain, and she could tell she was losing Vivi. But she needed the drama spelled out. Quinn was far too removed from high school high jinks to "get it."

"Well, yeah. But his dad was going to kill him, so he needed, like, a scapegoat."

Quinn startled beneath her covers, shocked at this. "Wait a minute. Mayor Van Holt—Dominic's *father* believes *you* are responsible for this so-called cheating?"

"Yes," Vivi whispered. "And you can't tell anyone. You have to swear, Mom."

"Wait a minute, wait a minute." Quinn reached for the bedside lamp and flipped it on.

Vivi winced and moaned. "*Ow*, Mom. Turn it *off*."

Flipping it back off, Quinn propped herself on her elbow. "You mean you took the fall, Vivi? That's why you're *here*? What—running from trouble that *you* aren't responsible for?"

Vivi grumbled her reply. "Dad is the only other person who knows. I made him swear on my grave that he wouldn't tell."

"Why are you protecting that boy? This is ridiculous, Viv. You're compromising your *own* future for Dominic Van Holt?"

"I care about him, Mom! And his dad is the *mayor*. I, like, had no choice. And when I just played along, well, it made everything easier. Anyway, I can't get in any *real* trouble. It wasn't *my* test. It was Dom's. And anyway, he's already suffered enough. Lost his scholarship. Now he's stuck working at the marina all summer and going to a community college. *Maybe*." Vivi's voice shook with emotion, but Quinn didn't know if it was heartache or worry or *what*.

"Viv," Quinn whispered, "this is silly. Your dad can fix it for you. I'm sure the mayor would *want* the right thing. Right? I mean—what on earth is he thinking? That his son walks on water? Did they check the phone number? Trace it to the real culprit?" A grown man acting like a teenager and her daughter acting like a martyr. Quinn never would have seen *this* coming. Then again...

"Mom, the real culprit doesn't matter. None of it matters anymore!" She was raising her voice now. "It's over, Mom!"

"But Dominic is staying around in Birch Harbor. Working at the marina and looking into community colleges? Are you still *together*?"

"I mean..."

There it was.

The true motive for Vivi's cover-up. Unadulterated puppy love. Infatuation. The thing that had brought Quinn down, too. A need to be needed above all else.

"Vivi," Quinn said as gently as she could muster, "I'm calling the mayor tomorrow. You aren't taking the fall for this. I won't stand for it."

"Mom, *don't*. Please."

"You're—what? Going to stay with Dom? Pretend like he didn't throw you under the bus? Go along with his lie? Are you *crazy*, Vivi?"

Vivi hissed back, "What? You mean crazy like *you*?"

There was no response. Not a thing Quinn could say back. Her left eyelid twitched, and her stomach ached with stress. She told Vivi goodnight. They'd talk again in the morning.

It took what felt like two hours, but Quinn finally fell into a hard sleep. The sort of sleep that had her dreaming and drooling and dry-mouthed when she awoke to a slit of sunshine the next morning.

She turned to Vivi's bed, fumbling through her dreams to the memory of their conversation, nearly ready to just apologize and let her daughter *be*.

But she couldn't.

Vivi was gone.

35

ANNETTE

Annette awoke with a bad feeling.

She was slated to show two houses that day to the Becketts. One that was fifty thousand dollars above their budget and one that was a hundred thousand dollars above their budget.

Hey, a young couple could dream, couldn't they?

Meanwhile, Annette was left with her almost-middle-aged husband and lingering debt and a dwindling business and a too-high mortgage and—still, she dreamed, too.

She dreamed that life would carry forward for them. That in three short years she and Roman would be empty-nesters together, playing weekend hosts to friends. Bunco and mah-jongg and ugly sweater parties and New Year's Eve parties and everything that life could be for a couple who rolled over the hill and still had so much left.

But no.

She dragged herself downstairs, free of makeup, her hair standing on end, her favorite bathrobe—the threadbare one—smelling like musty laundry that had sat too long in the washing machine. She felt blah.

None of that, however, mattered once she hit the kitchen.

Roman was there, two mugs on the kitchen island. He still wore his pajamas, too. A rarity. Roman was the sort who maybe didn't *own* pajamas. He wore jeans for comfort and tennis shoes as house slippers. But there he was, in boxers and a white T-shirt. Barefoot.

Barefoot! Her Roman.

Steam lifted from the mugs, giving him a ghostly appearance. Annette stopped at the threshold between the hall and the kitchen and her hand flew to her mouth.

"Where's Elijah?"

Roman's face crinkled. "In his room? I think? The door was closed."

She narrowed her gaze on Roman then gave him another once-over. "Then who died?"

"What?" Roman's face turned to befuddlement. "Someone died?" He took a sip from his mug.

Annette let out a short laugh then joined him, at ease that he was doing one normal thing—mainlining caffeine. "You're in your pajamas. You have no shoes on. You poured me a cup of coffee. So, yeah. Who died?"

His hand glanced off the corner of his eyebrow as if he'd pieced together the joke. "No one." He shook his head, but no chuckle came. No smile. Just a grimace. "Sorry. Annette, hon, we need to—oh, geez. I hate to put it this way, you know I do. But we gotta talk about something, babe."

ANNETTE SHOULD HAVE SEEN it coming. Really, she should have. Something had to give. They couldn't go on in this perfect life without at least *one* income source. And while Roman was too proud to ask his parents for help, Annette's parents were too far out of the picture for her to cry to. And even if she did cry to either of them, they'd no doubt find the moment perfect for rubbing it all in her face. She'd married Roman Best, after all. *A joke*, is what her mother had called him. *Not a man's man*, according to her father.

Roman was not a joke, though. And he may not be a man's man, but he was *her* man.

That's why, when he revealed that they lost the office space—three months overdue on rent was one month too many—she didn't hate him. She didn't demand a divorce or tell him he was a loser.

Annette, despite herself, loved Roman. And they were in it together.

However, that didn't change the fact that *something* needed to change.

Something more than a half-cocked effort to list their house.

"So, what do we do now, Roman?" she asked once they'd both drained a second cup of coffee. Elijah still hadn't appeared downstairs, which was unusual for him. He wasn't much for sleeping in. Usually, he got his cereal and headed back upstairs to get ready for the day, much like his dad in that regard.

"Logically, we drop the price here and downsize more dramatically than we planned. Worst case scenario, that's what we do, Annie."

She shook her head. "Elijah has three more years. *Three* more years. We aren't uprooting him for the last bit of his time in Hills School District. He has friends and a part-time job."

"We can stay local," Roman reasoned.

"What do we need to do for Best on the Block?" she demanded, suddenly fierce with passion.

"What do you mean?"

Annette pushed her mug away, threaded her fingers together, and pinned them to the table. "To make it work. To make *money*, Roman. What do we do?"

"Annette," he replied, his tone growing testy, "we sell *houses*. That's what."

"I'LL BE FRANK," Annette began, wiggling the spare key from the lock that hung beneath the doorknob on the house at Dogwood Drive, "though the other property might have been your dream, this one could be your reality." What she didn't say was that in order for this particular house to be their reality, they'd have to come up with a better offer than they could likely afford to make. Still, it wasn't Annette's business to bring her clients down to earth.

Was it?

The Becketts smiled nervously back at her. Annette had already showed them the home on Birch Tree Boulevard, and they were both impressed and edgy. Edgy over the price and their own limitations.

Annette had taken this pair on, rather than Roman, who normally showed during the week. She'd done it because she *knew* the Becketts. They lived so nearby. They liked Annette. She liked them.

"Sometimes reality can turn into a dream," Elora said.

Annette smiled at her. "I like that. I might have to steal it." She said it earnestly, with a rueful look as she popped the door open and ushered Elora and Tad Beckett inside.

Elora smiled and gestured around the foyer. "It's a bit like ours now, right, Tad?"

"Well, we are just around the corner." He chuckled and shrugged.

Annette knew that when a homebuyer was in the market to move, they probably wanted a new area. Definitely a change of scenery. If it was an interior change they were looking for, Annette wasn't sure she could sell this couple on a nearby property that followed a similar build pattern.

"Are you hoping to find a new neighborhood?" she asked casually as they moved into the kitchen, an airy space outfitted much like her own, with diamond-flecked granite counters and a big white farmhouse sink, complete with a broad apron.

"No." Elora and Tad answered in unison then immediately laughed together.

Elora took the opportunity to explain. "I was telling Roman that we wish we could just tear down our current house and build something right on our lot. It's not a new location we want. It's a new house."

"And a bigger one," Annette added.

"Right." Elora circled her protruding belly with her hand. "I can't imagine raising three kids in a two-bedroom."

"But if you had a three- or four-bedroom, even if it

was in a house around the corner?" Annette led the witness.

"All we need is more space," Elora confirmed.

"But we aren't interested in adding on," Tad clarified. "We already had a contractor out. It'd be too expensive to be worthwhile. A bigger new house makes more sense, apparently." He shrugged, dumbfounded by the logistics of contractors and additions and equity.

"Sure, sure." Annette frowned and swallowed. She knew her goal. Her goal was to sell a house. Several, in fact. After all, they had listed their own home. It, too, would be out of the Becketts' budget by a mile. But then—could there be a way to make a deal? She worked up the courage to take the next step. "Roman says you've been preapproved for a specific loan price. I have it here." She glanced down at their client folder. "And you have a bit of a down payment."

"My parents," Elora offered meekly. "They're trying to help a bit, but it's not enough for an addition, I'll admit."

It was hardly enough for a down payment, truth be told. "So, you can step out of your projected budget a bit, as long as you can make the monthly payment on Tad's salary." She looked hard at Tad, who she expected would be further confused.

A mild expression crossed his face, like he wasn't quite aware of the rumor about public school teachers.

"If you don't mind staying in the neighborhood, then I think I might have another option for you. A way to stick around *and* upgrade *and* sell your house. All at once." Here it was. She could make them an offer, *or* they could make an offer on this house. There was nothing else available in town. At least, not in their preferred areas of town and not with three or more bedrooms. Annette saw a light.

"Go on," Tad said, laughing nervously.

Annette did. "I have another house we can look at. And it, too, is right around the corner."

Tad and Elora exchanged a look then both gave Annette a clear nod.

Game on.

Annette ended their current tour early. She withdrew her phone to warn Roman and Elijah that she was bringing visitors. It wasn't yet ten o'clock. Elijah had better wake up. But just as she pulled her phone from her purse, she saw a stack of unread text messages, all from within the last fifteen minutes.

Alarmed, Annette excused herself from the Becketts and turned away, opening each message to see an increasingly panicked story development.

Vivi had, apparently, run away.

36

JUDE

J ude slept in the day after the interview and the job offer. The day after her whole life had changed.

Well, she hadn't really *slept* in. She lay in. Languidly and sumptuously, flipping through a magazine idly and daydreaming. Excitement filled her chest. Motivation. Rejuvenation. All because of her imminent return to the classroom, once again as Ms. Banks. Not quite *Miss* this time. Not as Mrs. Carmichael, either, though. It was a good middle ground for a teacher. The mystique.

She hadn't taught in years upon years, but she'd grown to miss it. Not so much the work, which she found at times tedious, but the purpose. The students, too. Though, admittedly, this was an aspect of teaching that set Jude apart. For she didn't often see her students as the sweet cherubs that other teachers—better teachers?—did. She saw them as what they were: her charge.

Too excited and impatient to revisit the roots of her educational philosophy, Jude set that aside. She had other business to attend to first. Quinn's house. And maybe she could share her good news with her new friends. Annette and Elijah would like to know. Maybe Jude would have Elijah in class? Maybe Annette would tell the PTSO about her hire and they'd put together something of a welcome basket? Those sorts of things were the little perks of the job—knowing people. Getting treats. The special elements.

After finally getting herself ready—it was after ten—Jude fed Liebchen, who purred disgruntledly that her servant was leaving her yet *again*. Too bad Hills High didn't allow class pets. Then again, Liebchen would never tolerate such a role. She was a feline, not a gerbil.

Once Liebchen purred contentedly at her dish, Jude headed to Quinn's, a lightness in her step and a fresh-brewed travel mug of coffee in her grip.

"Jude!" Annette waved frantically from her porch. Jude all but laughed to herself. She was growing to like this street. The nosiness had turned to friendliness in just a matter of weeks—a month or so. How a person's circumstances could change so quickly was a truth not unfamiliar to Jude, of course.

"Morning!" Jude called back. "You two ready?" Her own tone came out strange to Jude. Airy and breezy and sweet. She went with it.

But even from Jude's spot down on the sidewalk, she could see a shadow cross Annette's face. Her smile slipped away. Perhaps she wasn't smiling to begin with? She looked left then right, then back into the house, then left the porch and jogged—*yes, jogged!*—to where Jude stood.

"Haven't you heard?"

"Heard what?" Jude frowned and glanced around as if to brace for an attack.

For the first time, Jude saw that Annette was dressed to the nines—looking like she'd stepped fresh off the Dillard's exhibit touting the new line of women's pantsuits. Like she'd come from work. Jude hadn't realized Annette was going *into* work. Certainly not to show houses. Not to the office. She'd been home quite a lot.

Then, it occurred to Jude that she hadn't checked her phone since the night before. It still lay attached to its charger on her kitchen counter. Lately, this had become her habit. With so few people in touch with her, she'd replaced late-night scrolling with early evening reading and television in bed. The change had

done her good, but now she feared she'd missed something important. Something critical.

And she was right.

Annette's face was painted over in fear.

"No one can find Vivi."

37

BEVERLY

After all that, Principal Darry Ruthenberg had declined the interview.

Not, however, for any reason that Beverly would have expected. He said he'd be happy to talk about the school. Just not with her.

Not *yet*.

This, naturally, sent her reeling. She flew back to the office, ignoring Forrest there and grabbing her bags and going home, where she sank into the sofa and sobbed. Hard. For a long time.

When the tears drained out of her body, leaving her as shriveled and dry as a prune, sleep came. Fitfully.

She awoke the next morning with a raging headache and a phone choked with missed calls and texts.

Had to be Darry, of course. And Forrest, too. Both apologizing, maybe. She had nothing to say to either one of them, but especially not to Darry. He should know that she was at the school to handle business, nothing more and nothing less. And for him to suggest that she wasn't ready? Bold and indecent. Bold and *indecent*.

Ignoring her phone's blinking blue light from its position on the floor near her dangling hand, she rolled over on the couch and pulled a pillow onto her face.

Her temples throbbed. The hollow spot at the base of her neck pulsed in pain. Her throat hurt. Everything *hurt*.

There was just one fix.

Coffee.

Dragging her aching body to the kitchen, Beverly blindly pawed for her coffee grinds. The ceramic scoop chimed hollowly within its matching jar. She peered inside. *Empty*.

Driving to The Nut House, Harbor Hills' one and only drive-through coffee spot, was positively out of the question. A drive into town would do nothing but exacerbate her emerging migraine.

She went to the garage, where canned foods and expired cereals collected dust on an aluminum shelf. Blankly studying the musty contents, she spotted a red-lidded coffee-sized tin toward the back. Brief hope propelled her forward, and she pulled it out.

Hot cocoa. A useless substitute.

An idea flickered in her mind. Her neighbors. Shamaine. Jude. Annette. Beverly. Even Quinn. One of them had to stock regular coffee. Or, at the very least, Diet Coke. Even Pepsi.

But then she'd have to *face* them.

The throbbing pulsed up the back of her head. There was no other choice. Not even a shower could come before coffee. Not today.

Fifteen minutes later, she was dressed as much as possible—black leggings and an oversize blue T-shirt —and wandered out of her house and next door, ringing Jude's doorbell then rubbing circles into either side of her forehead.

After half a minute, there was no answer. No movement, even. Not even the fluffy tail of Jude's massive cat waved in the window.

Beverly moaned to herself and swung around, shielding her eyes from what little sun made its way up to Jude's front porch.

She turned back and gave the bell one more ring.

Another half a minute passed and nothing.

At last, Beverly worked up the energy to leave the porch and move toward the street, where she squinted through the sun and stared first at Shamaine's house. Bleh. Then Annette's. Double bleh.

Finally, Quinn's.

She was already due at Quinn's house to help prep for the yard sale. Quinn would be busy. Too busy to notice that Beverly looked like she'd barely survived a tornado.

Tenderly, she walked up the street to the cluttered drive, cutting directly through junk and stained furniture and up to Quinn's front door, which stood half-open already.

Frowning and forgetting just momentarily the ricocheting pounding in her neck and head, she opened the screen and stuck her head inside. Bold, maybe, but Beverly was growing desperate by degrees. "Quinn?" she called weakly, only to send a searing shot of agony up the center of her forehead and to the top of her skull.

She heard voices in the depths of the house, but no one answered her call.

Fed up—with herself, with the headache, and with the fact that no one was standing at their door with a steaming cup of coffee outstretched to her—Beverly pushed inside and made her way down the hall and toward the kitchen, in the direction of the voices.

Focusing every last bit of energy on stepping lightly so as not to shake the rocks in her head, she finally arrived at the doorway to the kitchen. Closing her eyes for a moment, she opened them again and started her apology. "I am so sorry to intrude, Quinn, but—"

Her vision cleared and she saw that Annette and Jude stood huddled at the island. In the far corner was Quinn, turned away, a beige telephone cord wrapped around her back and her ex-husband standing sentinel at her side.

Adjusting her focus back to Jude and Annette, Beverly cocked her head. "What's going on?"

Jude and Annette answered in tandem. A brittle, lifeless synchronization. "Vivi is missing."

38

QUINN

As soon as she'd woken up to discover her daughter's bed empty and the small room at Bertie's devoid of her things, Quinn had figured Vivi fled, somehow, to Birch Harbor.

No, she didn't suspect a kidnapping. No, she didn't suspect foul play, even.

In her heart of hearts, she knew that Vivi had left willfully. Because it's the sort of thing Quinn herself had done, too. And not just once, either. Over and again. When things got hard, when she couldn't control her circumstances in *just* the right way and with *just* the right degree of comfort, she, too, fled.

But when Quinn got in touch with Matt, he had no clue what she was talking about. Vivi hadn't gone "home." Not to Birch Harbor.

Neither had she made it to any of her friends' houses there.

Matt called the Birch Harbor police. Quinn called the Harbor Hills police. County officials were preparing for a broad-scale search, and this turned Quinn's stomach.

Where else could Vivi be?

Where else did she have to go?

Nowhere, of course.

Matt joined Quinn at the Apple Hill house, and by then, most of the town knew to be on the lookout for a dangerously pretty blonde teenager.

At the top of the list of interest locally was Elijah, Vivi's only known peer contact.

The police had him now, in the backyard, while Quinn called every single person in her life to beg for any information they could possibly have.

After she finished talking to her brother, who knew nothing, she turned back to her kitchen, broken.

"You really didn't wake up?" Matt accused.

A gag crawled up Quinn's throat. "I'm gonna be sick." She dashed to the kitchen sink where dry heaves racked her body.

Hands rubbed her back, but surely, they weren't her ex's hands. Oh, no. If they weren't already divorced before, she could be sure that they'd be divorced after this. Quinn didn't care about that. She cared about her daughter and the fact that she was in the exact same spot she'd found herself before. On the outs. Just when things were going well, she had to go and ruin it all over again. Although, to be fair, some of this ruin began elsewhere. Quinn had just picked it up and carried it forward.

"Think, Quinn. Is there anywhere *here* she might be?" Matt demanded.

"I can send Elijah to the movie theater after his interview," Annette offered helpfully. "I mean, I doubt there's anything playing this early, but that's a teen sort of hangout. Right? Maybe she just wanted an escape. We all need an escape sometimes."

Matt blew air through tight lips, effectively shutting her down.

"The police are going to canvass—oh *my*—" Quinn choked down a sob at the word. She swallowed hard, willing her voice to cooperate. "They are going to check every house in this area. But she doesn't know anyone in Crabtree Court. The only place she's been, really, is here." Quinn covered her face in her hands, rubbing her eyes hard.

"How long do you think she's been gone?" Jude asked quietly.

Quinn shrugged. "We went to bed late. I was awake even after that for a while, I think. Probably early morning. Very early." She glanced at her wristwatch. "It's almost eleven, so that's *hours*."

"Did you have an argument?" Matt asked, panic

streaking his voice as he pushed his hands through his hair.

Quinn squeezed her eyes shut. They had too much of an audience for her to be honest. "Not an argument, no." She shook her head. "But she told me what happened."

Her revelation was met with quiet.

Her neighbors—her *friends*—took the hint. "I'm going to call Roman," Annette declared, leaving the room with her phone in her hands.

"I'll—um—I have contacts in Birch Harbor. The town council. The mayor—surely he can pull some strings," Jude said.

Cringing, Quinn shot her a look. "Thanks. That'd —that'd be fine."

"No," Matt interjected.

Quinn glared at him. "What?"

"I already talked to Van Holt." He turned his gaze on Quinn. "*And* Dominic."

"*Well?*" Quinn demanded.

"She's not there. They haven't heard from her. And the police know now."

"About the—"

Matt gave a curt nod. "Yes." Then he waved his hand dismissively. "It's irrelevant."

Quinn's stomach turned to knots. She had gotten her way. Vivi would be livid.

Now wasn't the time to pester Matt for details or

accuse him of being slow on the uptake. Of handling everything wrong. Clearly, neither one of Vivi's parents was well enough equipped to parent her *correctly*. Something had to change.

Annette burst back into the kitchen. "Possibly unrelated," she said loudly, panting. "But Roman just got home. Sadie is missing, too."

"Sadie?" Quinn's chest heaved in another round of nausea, even though she had no idea what a dog's absence could mean.

"Our dog—" Annette started.

Just then, the back door opened. Elijah stepped in, his head lowered, hands in pockets. Behind him, one of the two cops who had taken him out there was ushering him inside.

Quinn sensed something had shifted in this early stage of the search.

When Elijah's face lifted from his chest, Quinn saw that it was tear-streaked and blotchy. His lips quivered as he managed to say, "I'm so sorry, Ms. Whittle." Then, to his mother. "I'm sorry, Mom."

39

QUINN

Quinn broke away from the kitchen and tore across Annette's backyard to the fort at the far corner. She ignored her friends and the police officer who'd prompted Elijah to make his confession, instead frantic to go and see if what he'd said was true.

Matt was hot on her heels, but as they neared the little scene—now crawling with a fresh handful of officers, as well as Roman Best—she spied her daughter.

Vivi crouched at the opening of the fort, her grip on Sadie's collar tight. Desperate. Her face, like Elijah's, was red-stained and fearful. "Mom?" she asked through a crack in the people surrounding her.

Quinn rushed in, wrapping her arms around Vivi, who let go of the dog's collar and squeezed back.

"Viviana Fiorillo, what *happened*?" she whispered in her daughter's ear.

Satisfied that Vivi had done exactly what the skeptical Special Victims Unit folks had expected she had done, the police cleared out as quickly as they'd crowded in. Their quick work and heavy force was not necessarily as much of a testament to the high stakes of Vivi's sudden disappearance, as it was a testament to the slow life of Harbor Hills.

Quinn was glad of that.

Vivi was not.

Now, they were back in the kitchen in Quinn's nearly empty house. Quinn stood at the stove, brewing a pitcher of iced tea, keeping her hands as busy as possible. Matt paced the hall, calling everyone back in Birch Harbor to share the news. The neighbor ladies curled themselves around the kitchen island, chatting excitedly at Vivi.

Elijah went home to suffer the wrath of his father. To be fair, Matt was angry, too. It was a father's job to uphold the pressure, after all.

It was Annette who first broke through with the hard questions. "Vivi, sweetheart, did Elijah talk you into this?"

"No!"

"Did he *meet* you?" Annette pressed.

Vivi shook her head and worked her lower lip in her teeth. "He picked me up."

"He *drove*?" Quinn asked.

Annette was even more aghast. "He hasn't even taken driver's ed yet!"

"I'm sorry," Vivi whined. "I told him it was a secret." She looked down at her lap. "I made him swear to be quiet. I just...I just needed *space*."

Quinn sighed. "Was this a—some sort of cry for attention, Viv?"

Vivi's mouth puckered. "*Mom*," she groaned, glancing awkwardly at the other two women. The third one, Beverly, had just popped two aspirin and filled a plastic drinking cup with yesterday's cold black coffee. Then she had seen herself out. Now that things had settled, Quinn was thankful at least *one* of them had somewhere better to be.

But Jude quickly got the hint. "We'll leave you two. But we can come back. Tonight, or at the crack of dawn—"

"That's right," Annette agreed. "The yard sale. Do you want me to cancel, Quinn?"

Quinn shook her head. There was no way she'd give up all their progress. "Come early, please. I'll be up at five, if not before then."

Annette and Jude nodded and started to go, but Quinn added one last thing. "And both of you—*thank you*. For being here for us. For me." A weak smile lifted her cheeks, and they returned it before leaving for good.

Now it was just Quinn, Vivi, and Matt. And Matt was finally off the phone.

"You're coming back, I guess," Matt said to their daughter, blowing out a sigh. "I thought bringing you here would clean up your first mess. Not create another."

"Matt," Quinn tsked. "The first 'mess' had nothing to do with Vivi."

He scowled and dipped his chin to the teenager. "Is that what you told her?"

Vivi paled. "I told her the truth."

"The truth is, Vivi isn't allowed to date," Matt said. "Isn't that right, Quinn?"

Quinn and Matt were no experts at coparenting. But they'd agreed on this point, which was why when Vivi's relationship became public knowledge, there had been family conflict. Dancing around how to manage Vivi's growing interest in boys while being responsible parents and *reasonable* ones.

"That's true. And when you started dating Dominic, you knew you were edging toward the line."

"What line?" Vivi asked.

"The line of good decisions versus bad ones," Quinn replied softly. Then she looked at Matt. "But that has nothing to do with what Dominic Van Holt pulled." Then her eyes switched back on Vivi. "Right?"

Matt folded his arms. "What exactly happened, Vivi? Because when I spoke to the mayor, he seemed to believe you played a pivotal role. He even thought your running away was linked."

"It wasn't me." Vivi winced. "It was Mercy."

"Mercy? Mercy Hennings?" Matt roared. "No *way*."

Mercy was Vivi's best friend and a sugar-sweet counterpart. For all of Vivi's strength, Mercy softened her. And for all of Mercy's weakness, Vivi hardened her. They were salt and pepper, but there were two things that the duo shared: a scary-high intellect and missing mothers.

Quinn crumpled into the chair next to her daughter. "Did you talk her into it?"

"I—" Vivi flashed a look at her dad. "No. Dom texted me during the test, and I showed it to Mercy. I didn't tell her he'd started the test. She thought he was reviewing some math formulas before it started. That's all it was. She texted back quickly, hit send, and that was *it*. Mom, I swear. Dad," Vivi begged.

"You lied to me," Quinn pointed out. "Then you ran away. Everyone in town was looking for you. Some people thought you were abducted, Viv. This is a *huge* deal. And it started with a stupid text during the SAT?" Quinn looked hard at Matt. "That's why Vivi is here?

Because you think she got the mayor's son in big trouble?"

Matt joined them at the counter, falling onto his elbows on the table and pushing his hands through his hair. Seeing him there, despairing and vulnerable, it made him seem like a brother to Quinn. A cousin. A friend. Someone who *was* on her team, even if they didn't share the romance that had started it all. He cleared his throat and lowered his voice. "She's here, Quinn, because she needs you."

40

QUINN

I took a little effort to get Matt to give them one-on-one time. But eventually, he assented and saw himself to the front yard, finding a mottled Georgian armchair to relax in.

Inside, Quinn and Vivi sat at the kitchen island, which was fast becoming Quinn's refuge in that house in shambles on that nosey strip of Crabtree Court. The shambles house that was fast becoming some version of a *new* house on Apple Hill Lane.

"Viv, I know this will sound selfish or biased or *whatever*, but your dad is right."

"About what?" Vivi had slumped halfway onto her stool, an unintentionally industrial-chic metal thing that didn't match the wooden one on which Quinn sat. Maybe eclectic would end up being her décor style.

"You need me. And honestly? I need *you*." She

blinked once then rubbed her eyes to keep from blinking twice more.

"Last time I lived with you, you made me shower before I went to bed," Vivi pointed out coldly. "You said my bed was for sleeping not sitting. You wouldn't let my friends hang out on it."

Quinn's jaw tensed. She swallowed, the skin on her face feeling dry and taut like her skeleton needed to rip out of it to be free. She needed that. To be free. Of the compulsions. The obsessions. The control.

This house was supposed to be the first step, and it was a good one. Then Vivi came back, and Quinn felt like that was an omen, and she got better. Really, she did.

But could a mild improvement undo years of damage? Years of breaking the one relationship in her life that mattered?

"I won't do that anymore, Viv," she whispered, ashamed.

"I got sick with the flu, and I lay down on the sofa, and you made me move because it was a sitting sofa. Unlike the bed." Vivi's tone remained icy, and her words were carefully formed. As if she'd been planning this...this *lecture*. "Then you buy *this place*." Vivi lifted her hand and made a face. "And when I got here, I was like, *What? Why would she buy a place like this when I couldn't even sit on my bed or lie down on the sitting sofa?*" Vivi looked her mother in the eye. "What does this house have that changed you? What does *this* place have that I don't?"

Quinn's face fell.

She'd earned this, but that didn't lessen the jolt of heartache. She smoothed her shirt against her abdomen. Then repeated the gesture twice more, then blinked three times.

Her voice shook as she replied. "I'm working on it, Viv. I bought this house so that I'd knock it off. Exposure therapy. I'm working on my problems. I want to be better, not even for me, but for *you*. I hope you can see that, but if you can't—I understand." It was the only thing Quinn could say. What more was there?

"Dad thinks I need you, but does he even know?"

"Know what?" Quinn asked, frightened of her daughter's clear vision.

"That you do that stuff." Vivi pointed to Quinn's fingers as they tapped a pattern on the tabletop.

She stopped immediately, studying her blunt nails then the pads of her fingers as if they were foreign objects. "Yes."

"Is *that* why you divorced?"

Quinn considered this. "No." She smiled sadly then snorted half a laugh at herself. The situation. "Your dad is better than that."

Vivi's face twisted in confusion.

Letting out a long sigh, Quinn explained. "He knew about my OCD, sure. It was even worse when we first met, if you can believe that." She raised an eyebrow, and Vivi copied her, then cracked a reluctant grin. Quinn went on. "He didn't really mind that. And I didn't mind his obsession with work, either. Now that I think about it, Matt's the other half of the reason I got this place."

"Huh?" Vivi's face crinkled further.

"Yeah. I learned a lot about home improvement from your dad. But I digress. We weren't meant for each other. That was it. He had another love." Vivi blinked. She already knew what Quinn meant. *Who.* But Quinn smiled earnestly. "It's okay, Viv. Really. So did I."

"You had another love?"

"You, my dear." Quinn twisted and cupped her daughter's face in her hands. "Listen. I know it's not... ideal—what we've had. But you have three years left of school. We could make them count. You could let me rewind. Make it up to you."

"And I guess I could make it up to you."

Quinn's mouth twitched. She swallowed. "Make *what* up to me?"

"Everything I've done wrong, too," Vivi replied sheepishly. "Choosing Dad. Lying about Dominic. Running away like an attention-seeker." Her face fell and her chin dropped down to her chest. "Like a brat."

"Hey, we all have those moments."

"You ran away?" Vivi glanced at her mom from

beneath her bare blond eyelashes. She looked younger without makeup. Sweeter. More like the little girl Quinn had fussed over for so, so long. And yet so fleeting a spell. That was motherhood, though. The long days. The short years.

Quinn nodded. "Many times. I've been running away since I was younger than you." She cracked a smile. "It just never got the same amount of...attention, I suppose." She lowered her voice and leaned in. "Less dramatic."

Vivi giggled. A girlish giggle. One to match her faint eyelashes and her wispy, downy hair, and her foolishness, too. Quinn draped her arms around Vivi and pulled her in. Their barstools knocked together and wobbled, sending them both into laughter as they nearly toppled over.

Quinn undraped her arm, and they righted themselves. Then, they stood, and a fresh breath filled Quinn's lungs. Vivi inhaled, too.

"So, what's next?" Vivi asked.

Taking a deep breath, Quinn realized she didn't know the best thing. The best thing could be for Vivi to go back to Birch Harbor and face Dominic and Mercy and the mayor and live down the mess. The best thing could be to go back to Birch Harbor incognito and pretend it never happened. The best thing could be to move somewhere new and start over from scratch.

But Quinn was doing that now. For the both of them?

No.

To grow up, Vivi couldn't run. Not like Quinn had. Running only resulted in counting and worrying and showering until her skin was raw and—

"I'm back."

The voice came at the back door.

Elijah.

The other piece of the puzzle. The other thing Vivi still had to face. No matter where she went, maybe she'd be running. Maybe, Quinn thought, running wasn't so much a physical act as it was an emotional one.

Vivi spun to see him then looked back at her mom, who nodded and whispered, "You have to talk to him. You two were in on it together."

Narrowing her eyes back on the door, Vivi rose and smoothed her pajamas—she'd worn them when she left Bertie's, packing all of her things into her suitcase and hauling it out with her, undetected by the sleeping innkeeper and everyone else who might have been awake at that early hour.

"Elijah, did you really drive to Bertie's in the middle of the night to pick Vivi up?" Quinn asked as she strode to the door to let him in.

He shrugged.

Opening the door for Elijah, Quinn looked back at

her daughter. "Why hold Sadie hostage, though? That's what I don't get."

"I was wondering about that, too," Elijah said, a half grin creeping up the side of his face. He was undeniably adorable, and Quinn could see exactly why Vivi had been fast to latch on to him. Something in his eyes, in his way, was trustworthy. At least it was Elijah whom Vivi had called. Not Dominic.

"She kept, sort of, *frolicking* around. Barking at me and drawing attention," Vivi said. "I was still figuring out my next move, so I had to lure her in and rub her belly and convince her to just hang out with me. Without making a sound."

"You're good with dogs, I guess," Elijah pointed out. "I can't believe she didn't come to my dad when he called."

Vivi shrugged.

"Speaking of your next move," Quinn interjected. "Where *were* you going to go? What were you going to do?"

"I didn't know at first. Maybe I'd find a way to go to Birch Harbor, but then that would be dumb. I thought about hiding out at home—I mean *here*." The slip wasn't unnoticed by Quinn, and her eyes lit up at it. But Vivi went on, trying to pretend she hadn't just called the Carl Carlson hovel *home*.

"And then your sidekick gave you up?"

"No," Vivi said lamely.

Quinn furrowed her eyebrows. "What do you mean *no*?"

"I texted Elijah. I said it was over. He should 'find' me. But I guess they pulled him to interview right after. So, the jig was up." She smirked. "Anyway, I couldn't do to Elijah what I'd been accused of doing to Dominic."

"What's that?" Quinn asked.

"Get him in trouble."

Quinn watched Vivi and Elijah exchange an unreadable look. Something teenager-y and deceptive and innocent all at once.

"That's fair. And speaking of your Birch Harbor days, have you talked to Mercy? Made up with her?"

Vivi smiled widely. "She's the only other person who knows, and honestly? I think she likes having a little secret of her own." Vivi glanced down. "Although, I guess it's not a secret anymore." When she looked back up, there was a pensiveness to her eyes, like she was thinking about the meaning of life. "Mercy needed a little scandal. It was good for her. We'll always be best friends, no matter what. That, I know for a fact. The minute I got back in here, I texted her. She's already begging to come for a visit."

The implicated settled in the air. *Come for a visit.*

Quinn smiled. "She's welcome anytime. We've got the space." She held her arms out wide. "I have one last question, Viv. What made you decide it was over?

That it was time to surrender and stop hiding?" Quinn asked.

Vivi's eyes shifted dreamily to Elijah, who stood awkwardly by the sink, his hands stuck in his pockets, his hips twisting to and fro.

It came together, then. Vivi had found something in Harbor Hills. Something she wasn't looking for. Something she didn't necessarily *need*. But something *more* than a mom who counted to three and made her sit on the sitting sofa and keep her dirty shoes off the bed and then moved her into a dilapidated shack crawling over in mold and grime, undermining all those years of obsessive cleanliness.

Vivi had found another friend. Someone else who needed a bit of scandal, maybe. But someone whom she would never have to run from. Someone she could even run *to*.

The thing was?

Quinn was pretty sure she'd found that, too.

Her neighbors. The women of Apple Hill Lane.

41

VIVI

Convincing her dad that she could stay in Harbor Hills was easier than Vivi had predicted. He was nervous when he left, but not too nervous. Not that Vivi could tell.

She still had some amends to make, both in Birch Harbor and in Harbor Hills. In either place, it'd be embarrassing. She'd been silly to run away. Ridiculous. But if she hadn't, maybe she wouldn't have figured things out with her mom. Maybe that moment of brutal honesty would have stayed buried.

And anyway, Elijah didn't judge her.

He understood.

She liked that about Elijah. He had a family who looked perfect on the outside, but they were anything *but*. Kind of like Vivi.

And she and Elijah had something to share, too. A

little drama. They sort of thrived on it. It added that spark that all the best friendships had. Not that they needed much of a spark. Being friends with a boy was naturally thrilling. For Vivi, at least.

The running away thing—she knew she'd never live it down. Not fully. And that was why a spell inland might do her some good. Give her the space she thought she needed. She'd go back there. Of course, she would. Vivi might be a runner, but she wasn't a drifter. Not like her mom.

Oh, Quinn. The one person in the world Vivi couldn't figure out. Her own mother. The woman who gave birth to her. Who changed her name after the divorce and bobbed along in life, nitpicking Vivi and finding problems everywhere she went. Quinn needed someone to tie her down. Not a man, of course. Vivi wasn't a proponent of her mother using a man for stability. More likely, it was a calling for Vivi. And this worked, because, well, Vivi liked the other ladies on the street. She liked Elijah and his dad and Sadie. She liked that the house where she'd be staying had history —adventure. She liked being in a *real* town, where there was drama. Secrets. Gossip. All the stuff that gave Vivi excitement. The stuff that, ironically, could keep her out of trouble.

She liked it all.

What she liked best, though, was being with her mom.

THE YARD SALE was in full swing, her mom frantically trying to make decisions on what to keep and what to let go. She'd changed her mind. She found herself fond of some of the little trinkets and decorative pieces left behind. Choosing what she was most fond of, however, was harder than you'd think. Some of ol' Carl Carlson's belongings might have value. And some were in good enough shape to clean, repair, and hang on to.

The other ladies were all there helping. That was nice. Elijah came, too.

"Viv!" her mom cried out in the direction of the folding table where Vivi and Elijah were holding down the banker's box of change and dollar bills.

"Yeah?" She squinted through the morning sun.

"Can you grab a grocery bag and a wad of newspaper? He's taking the set of vases." Her mom gestured to an antsy-looking yard-saler who held a glass vase in each hand. Carl Carlson had dozens of the things. You'd think he'd had a wife who kept flowers. But no. Carl Carlson was as single and depressing as they came.

"Here." Elijah grabbed a clump of the dusty old newspapers from the stack they'd dragged out for just this occasion.

Vivi took it, thanked him, grabbed a spare bag, and delivered both to her mother before returning to her chair and the doughnut that sat in front of her. She took another bite, her eyes lingering on the top of the stack of newspapers that stood between her and Elijah.

"Hm," Vivi murmured through a mouthful. She frowned and leaned down closer to the front page.

"What?" Elijah leaned over, too, and they bumped heads.

Vivi laughed, rubbed her head, and reeled back, swallowing her bite then pointing to the article. "The reporter's name was Beverly."

"Yeah?"

"Like our neighbor. Beverly. She's a reporter."

"This is really old, though," Elijah pointed out.

Vivi looked at the date and did the math quickly. "The year I was born." Then she looked at Elijah. "You, too." They had already exchanged birthdates. A natural step in growing a friendship.

He shrugged, unfazed.

Vivi read the headline aloud. "Missing Detroit Woman Had Ties to Harbor Hills."

Elijah returned his gaze to the paper, then grabbed it and moved it to the table, smoothing it out so they could both pore over the juicy story.

Just as he'd finished reading, a woman's voice interrupted them.

"Sorry to bother you two."

Vivi looked up, and she felt the blood drain from her face. "Oh, hi."

Beverly.

Vivi pursed her lips to keep from a mischievous smile toward Elijah, who cleared his throat.

"Vivi, your mom said to bring this over. I'm donating it for the sale. You have the price stickers, I guess?"

Beverly's eyes were sad, her tone uneven, like she might cry.

Discreetly, Elijah folded the newspaper and tucked it back onto the stack—upside down, Vivi noticed.

Vivi accepted Beverly's item. An unopened box of fairy lights. "Oh my gosh," Vivi gushed. "I've always wanted these in my bedroom."

"Really?" Beverly's face lifted a little. She smiled. "They were for—they were a gift. But I never got the chance to give them."

Vivi knew about Kayla. Elijah had told her everything. A lump formed in her throat, and she felt inexplicably sad now, too. She didn't know the girl. She didn't even know Beverly, but here the woman was, passing over her deceased daughter's presents.

It about killed Vivi. "How much do you want for it?" she asked.

Beverly shook her head. "Oh, I don't care. The money goes back to your mom. You decide."

"Well, could I maybe...*keep* them?" It was a bold question. Too bold. Inappropriate. Vivi squeezed her eyes shut. "I'm sorry. That's so rude of me. I—"

"That would be wonderful. You can take them home to Birch Harbor. Hang them up and send me a picture." This time, Beverly's smile reached her eyes, crinkling them.

"Maybe," Vivi said, her gaze shifting to Elijah then back to Beverly. "Or maybe I can hang them in my bedroom here?"

As if on cue, Quinn came up behind Vivi, resting her hands on her shoulders. "Did Vivi tell you guys?"

"What?" Elijah twisted, his mouth falling open as he waited for Quinn to come out with it.

Beverly cocked her head, her sadness now suspended, it appeared.

Vivi's chest inflated, and her skin buzzed to life. Her entire body filled with the hope she had for the next three years. For what was to be. For the opportunities and the changes and the *adventure*. The weekend visits from Mercy and weekend trips to the little lakeside town that had been her home for just one bittersweet year.

"I'm staying in Harbor Hills."

1973

"How long will I stay here?" she asked Nana during supper that first night at 696 Apple Hill Lane. The question was bold and teetered on rude, she knew. But it was important. Where she wound up was *important*.

"You'll stay until we figure something out." It was Grandad who answered. A sputtering cough left spittle on his lip, which he wiped with a cloth napkin. His reply didn't mean she'd stay for good, apparently. But it didn't mean she'd leave, either.

After supper, she was excused to go upstairs, where she'd been shown the bathroom and the bedroom she could use. *Until they figured something out.*

Stopping first at the bathroom, the girl disrobed awkwardly, embarrassed to undress in a place so unfamiliar. So unwelcome, too.

Her pendant hung on her neck, the one remnant of what was now, officially, her old life. She clutched it, grappling with the past and the present and how the two had collided into *this*. This beautiful home on Apple Hill Lane in another town. With strangers for family.

She turned to the bathtub to find no showerhead. Just a porcelain, clawfoot basin, like she was in a palace or something.

Turning on the faucet, she waited for warm water. It came after a brief struggle. She bent over the edge, situated the stopper, then dipped her toes in, tentative, before settling the rest of her body.

Within ten minutes, a cry came from beyond the door. "Are you decent!"

Nana. A severe woman, she'd come to learn. Grandad was less severe. Not soft, but *nicer*. Kind of.

"Oh!" was all she could manage at first, embarrassed to be thought of as luxuriating. She ripped the plug from the bottom of the basin and stood with a jerk, unaware that the chain around her neck had caught on the faucet and snapped, and the pendant had slid off, circling the drain with the dregs of her first bath in a foreign tub.

The plunk of the silver into the shallow water ripped her attention from the door.

Panicked and aware of her total bareness now, the

girl squatted back down, clearing water from the drain like a person possessed.

But it was too late. The pendant was gone.

The door behind her swung open. She covered herself and crouched low.

Nana's voice returned, but she averted her gaze, respectful if awkward. "I just wanted to tell you. There is one school nearby. Makes sense you'll start Monday."

The girl frowned, confused. "Am I staying in Harbor Hills, then? For good?"

The woman gave a sigh. "No."

It would turn out, however, that Nana was wrong. All wrong.

That misnamed stretch of small town, in one way or another, would belong to this girl. This pitiful girl with a checkered past whose pendant had slithered down the drain and who wouldn't live in 696 just then. Not for long. Oh, no. But she *would* be back. To the house on Apple Hill Lane. Somehow. In some way.

EPILOGUE

Quinn, dressed in a red tank top and her white jeans, sauntered down her now-clear driveway, admiring the magic that was her new-old home. The yard sale had turned enough money to help cover some other, unforeseen repairs. Quinn even had some left over to treat the girls—she now called her neighbors *the girls* —for a night out for dinner and drinks.

In the days after, Vivi and Elijah spent their free time helping her clean, repair, and arrange the furniture and décor she'd salvaged from ol' Carl Carlson. In the end, she turned up with a mostly furnished house in working order. And, most importantly, it was so clean you could eat off the floor. Out of the tub, even!

Still, after salvaging what they could selling the rest, there remained heaps of things Quinn hesitated to part with. Call it instinct, but the stacks of newspapers, the boxes of paperwork...they felt *too important to toss*.

Jude agreed first. *What if they found something interesting?*

Beverly had agreed second, urging Quinn even more enthusiastically than Jude. *You never know* what *people leave behind when they die. There could be cash hidden in those stacks!*

Annette even offered up Elijah's mancave as a storage facility for all the paper stuff, in case there were certain legal documents worth saving.

Quinn figured the girls' efforts to help her save everything came each from a selfish motive. Jude, because she was, in many ways, like Carl Carlson— struggled with letting go. Beverly, because she also struggled to let go but *more* because she wanted a juicy story. And Annette, because she was a gossip, naturally. And any fodder for gossip was worth its weight in gold to Annette.

Quinn caved and stowed much of the boxes and the newspapers in the garage, thinking about them every moment of downtime she could steal between continuing to fix up the place and logging hours at the *Herald*.

Today, though, she had a true break. A holiday. It was the Fourth of July, and Apple Hill Lane was abuzz with celebration.

She strode to Annette's table, where she filled a cup

with ice and lemonade and curled it into her body, twisting around to take in the turnout.

Everyone in town had come, which made no sense. This was supposed to be a Crabtree Court block party, after all. So, what was her new boss doing there?

She turned back to Annette, who was chomping on baby carrots slathered in ranch dip. "Forrest Jericho is here," she said.

Annette gave her a look of surprise. "Well, yeah," she answered through a full mouth.

Quinn glanced left then right, as if searching the air around her for the obvious explanation. "*Why?*"

"He always comes to events with Beverly. She can't get rid of him."

This felt like a dangerous area to probe, but Quinn had to know. "Are they—" She gave Annette *the eyes*.

Annette cackled loudly. "Oh, *heavens* no! Forrest is her *cousin!*"

Quinn choked on her lemonade, coughing to the side until she recovered enough to laugh along with Annette. "Wow! She never mentioned it."

"Probably figured you knew. That's sort of how it goes around here. Everyone knows everything about everyone, so everyone *assumes* everyone knows everything about everyone. And anyway, she's... well...distracted."

"I get that," Quinn answered more soberly.

"And it seems like he is, too," Annette added, elbowing Quinn sharply in the side.

She winced briefly and was about to, again, ask for clarification, until her gaze settled on an oncoming figure.

"Quinn!"

Quinn turned, red-faced, to Annette, but she'd disappeared like a rabbit into a black top hat. Blinking three times, she felt her mouth for errant lemonade before smoothing her shirt—three times—and responding to him.

Grinning, she said, "Hi, Forrest."

ANNETTE PRACTICALLY DASHED over to Elijah and Vivi who had with them Vivi's friend, Mercy. The trio was too adorable, and she couldn't resist snapping a candid photo as they chatted like mini adults.

Elijah moaned and groaned at her, but the girls played along.

She studied the picture on her phone, catching something glinting off of Vivi's chest. A medallion, it appeared. With an...insignia? The little jewel ruined the photo, drawing a glare. "One more!" she trilled back, positioning her phone at an angle to avoid the sun. She snapped then looked again. "Perfect!"

"Annie," came Roman's voice. "You have a minute?"

She turned from the kids to see that he was standing with the Becketts. "Elora! Tad! Oh, I am *so* happy to see you here." Her eyes widened at Elora's form. "You're about to *pop*, honey!"

"I *know*. I'm terribly hot and uncomfortable, and I *definitely* won't stay long."

Tad reached around her back and rubbed it. "The mortgage company reached out just yesterday," he said, rocking Lincoln's stroller with his free hand. "Everything is in order. All we need is the final inspection," he said triumphantly.

Annette forced a smile even though a sick feeling curled up her insides. "Oh, right!" She turned to Roman. "So, you're not going to waive it, then?" She had figured they would. Especially after the screaming deal they were getting on Annette and Roman's house. Then again, the sale was traditional, in the end. Not sold *as is*. After all, *as is* would draw attention. Annette was sure she'd rather have a quick inspection than be the focus of neighborhood gossip. She could hear the questions now. *Why as is? That house is perfect! She could get twice what she's asking! Why would the Bests settle like* that? *Weren't they supposed to be the Best on the Block? Ha!*

"My parents said we'd better get the inspection. Just in case," Elora answered meekly.

"Roman." Annette turned to her husband, running her manicured hand down his Tommy Bahama button-up tee. "Do you want to have Dean handle it? He does inspections, you know. Or—?"

"Oh, we're going to get our own. Third party. That's what my parents say is best," Elora announced before shrinking back in on herself.

Her smile melting at the edges, Annette tried hard to stabilize it. The one thing she and Roman had not thoroughly discussed after her big idea to do a house swap was the *inspection*.

And, namely, what it would reveal.

"Let's talk about it tomorrow. After the festivities," Annette suggested, narrowing her eyes again on Elora's belly. "When you're feeling better."

And after Annette had time to make a plan.

JUDE AND BEVERLY stood together by the firecracker station. One per kid until it was time for the fireworks show, then they'd give out the rest. Spent watermelon rinds sat on each woman's plate, and Jude felt bloated and happy.

Beverly seemed more chipper, too. She'd had a margarita from the margarita station. It likely helped take the edge off.

Jude recalled the summer before, seeing Beverly, Tom, and Kayla all together for the affair on Main

Street. They'd been a model family. Happy and easy and beautiful, all of them.

As a leftover, Beverly hadn't quite upheld that beauty. Even today, decked out in a pretty blue blouse and white Bermuda shorts with pristine white-and-beige wedges, there was a lingering hollowness to her.

"How's your article going?" Jude asked between raucous children buzzing past.

Beverly's face opened. "Oh, it's—slow. I'm having a hard time getting to the main source I need to finish the series."

"Who's that?" Jude asked.

"Darry Ruthenberg. The principal."

"You were in his office last week," Jude pointed out.

"He turned me down," Beverly answered mildly. "I guess he's not ready to talk to the Widow of Hills High."

Jude lifted an eyebrow at Beverly, only to see a smirk cross the woman's face. It was a...joke? "Oh. Well, I'd be happy to give you a quote. Although, it'll probably do you little good. Depending on your angle."

"I'd happily take a quote. My angle isn't quite fleshed out. I'm trying to dig deeper, you know? Deeper than—*teachers die, teachers retire, teachers quit. Pay them more.*" Beverly flashed Jude a look. "Not that a higher salary will keep anyone from dying."

"It could keep us from retiring, though," Jude

answered. "Retiring and finding different, better-paying jobs."

It was Beverly's turn to lift an eyebrow. "You retired because of low wages? Initially, I mean?"

Jude shrugged. "People assume that private schools pay more." She looked directly at Beverly. "They *don't*. Anyway," she went on, "that was back when I had other things going for me."

Beverly frowned. "What do you mean?"

"Oh, you know. A generally functional marriage. The town council. Summer trips, winter trips. I had a life." Jude considered her wording and added, "I had a *different* life."

"Teaching will give you fulfillment, then?" Beverly prodded.

Jude nodded quickly. "Of course. I mean look at you," she said. "You've returned to reporting. And why? For the paycheck?"

The conversation had turned a little deeper than Jude expected, but maybe that was okay. She glanced across the cul-de-sac to see Quinn chatting with Beverly's boss. Nearby, along with two other couples, danced Annette and Roman. Country music blared from someone's speaker, and the dance floor was nothing more than a bare nook of asphalt up in the little cove by Shamaine's. But it was cute. To see that. To see couples in love. Maybe odd, too. Odd to see an affectionate middle-aged couple. Then again, maybe they weren't *quite* middle-aged. Not yet. Still odd. Good, but odd.

"I think everyone works for the paycheck," Beverly said. "But it's working after hours—that's when we work for the purpose."

People like that Dean Jericho character came to mind. The sort who worked with a purpose when he was on the clock. Like he was destined to do what he did. Maybe this assumption came from Jude's suspicion that the Jericho family was an old one. They'd probably been the first ones to bring electricity to Harbor Hills. And Forrest, too, had been given the *Herald* as an heirloom. All those Jericho boys were nothing more than local heartbreakers. The thought of Dean stirred something in Jude, but she tamped it down quickly. He was a fleeting moment in her summer. No more. No less.

Jude switched her mind back to Beverly's point; she tried to make sense of it. Maybe there could be a bit of balance in one's professional life: working for the paycheck and for the purpose. Still, was that what Beverly even meant?

Jude, herself, had applied to the school in order to make ends meet, true. But the rest of Beverly's assertion still confused her. "What do you mean?"

BEVERLY THREW a sidelong glance at Jude. "I mean..." She squeezed her eyes shut and shook her head. "I don't know what I mean." Then it came to her. "Well, I mean—it used to be, when I first started reporting, I'd be working a story at all hours. I was *obsessed* with it. It drove everything in my life. I was reading and studying around the clock. Facts became the structure to my day. Chasing down leads. Interviewing. Hounding people. I *lived* for it. And the paycheck was irrelevant. I'd have done it for free."

"So, what happened?" Jude asked.

Beverly didn't mind the question. She needed it. She needed it like she used to need those facts. Like lifeblood. Someone to talk to. Someone to confess to.

"What happened was," she said, a smile drifting across her mouth, "I had Kayla." Tears stung her eyes, and she swallowed *hard*, willing away the emotion. Today was supposed to be a good day. A fun day. Free of all that. She squinted through the sunlight to the margarita station. "I need another one of these." She held up her empty plastic cup, shaking the salty ice remnants.

"Let's go." Jude joined her, and they both indulged in a second drink.

After a few sips, Beverly said, "Did anything ever interrupt your work? Get in the way?"

Jude seemed thoughtful for a moment. Then, "Yes. Gene did. My marriage consumed me in a way school never could have. I suppose it was only because of our divorce that I can return in earnest."

"Yes. I get that," Beverly agreed. "But you probably don't have the guilt." She didn't mean it as an accusation. "I'm sorry." Beverly shook her head. "That was out of line, I—"

"No, I understand," Jude assured her. "You don't know if it's okay for you to turn your energy on something other than Kayla and Tom." Her voice was quiet and soft, and her words echoed in Beverly's brain.

She swallowed hard again, her nostrils flaring. "I just don't know what I should do. Or what I shouldn't do. It's like with my door—you know?"

"Your door?" Jude asked.

"When I painted it, that was a good day. Right? You know, I was feeling okay. Like it was something I could do for me. But the next day, I hated the sight of it. Why couldn't I just keep it natural oak, right? Tom liked the oak. Now I don't have that bit of him."

"At some point, Beverly, you have to move on and make these sorts of choices. Little choices that benefit you. Even if they don't honor their memory."

Beverly took a moment. She sucked in a deep breath and stared out at the party. People strolling and happy and normal. Annette and Roman, so in love. Quinn, talking to Forrest. Probably about work. Hah. The kids—Elijah and Vivi and their other friend— huddled conspiratorially and sort of meandering in

Beverly's general direction. Even after what had happened with Vivi, they were *okay*. That easiness eluded Beverly so. Her gaze landed on a surprisingly welcome sight. Darry Ruthenberg himself.

She looked at Jude and licked her lips. "I'm going to try again," she declared.

Jude followed Beverly's gaze as it returned to Darry, who'd come alone. He lived on Dogwood in a two-bedroom. Also alone. Just like Bev. Maybe she could start there, from a point of commonality. And then dig at the turnover rate. Find a way to turn an otherwise bland story into something juicy and wrought with the grit that small-town papers so often lacked.

Often, but not *always*.

"Yes, maybe he'll be a little more loose here. Rather than at school, where he probably needs to be professional." Jude was talking, but Beverly was only half listening. Her eyes had wandered up to Quinn's house. The next feature she'd take on.

"Jude," she said, quickly changing her mind. "What did you know about Carl Carlson?"

Jude's face turned stricken. "What do you mean?"

Beverly eyed the house again. "I think there's a story there."

"Oh, I doubt that." Jude said it with such finality. Such assertion that Beverly was nearly persuaded.

"Maybe not," Beverly agreed.

But she knew better.

Beverly knew that behind every confident, worry-free man or woman, there was a story.

There was a story behind Carl Carlson. There was a story behind Quinn. Behind Annette. Behind Jude.

And there was a story behind her, too. Behind Beverly.

All these stories of the people who lived on Apple Hill Lane. And no one who had ventured to tell those stories.

Until now.

Maybe her attempt to be near Kayla and Tom—by coming up with the school feature—was all wrong. Maybe there really was a better way to get close to them.

To honor their memory.

Maybe Beverly needed to find a new purpose. Something more than being the widow who lived in the house with the blue front door.

CONTINUE the saga with book two: *The House with the Blue Front Door*. Available where books are sold.

Stay in touch with the author. Visit elizabeth-bromke.com today.

ALSO BY ELIZABETH BROMKE

Harbor Hills

The House on Apple Hill Lane

The House with the Blue Front Door

The House Around the Corner

The House that Christmas Made

Birch Harbor

House on the Harbor

Lighthouse on the Lake

Fireflies in the Field

Cottage by the Creek

Bells on the Bay

Hickory Grove:

The Schoolhouse

The Christmas House

The Farmhouse

The Innkeeper's House

The Quilting House

Gull's Landing:

The Summer Society

ACKNOWLEDGMENTS

Elise Griffin, Beth Attwood, and Tandy Oschadleus—thank you each for your keen eye, careful notes, and your willingness to tackle my stories efficiently and thoroughly. You are miracle workers, each of you!

Jordan Black, this thank-you is a long time coming. Thanks so much for your willingness to answer hard questions about tough situations in life. You're wonderful.

My quilting bunch on Facebook—this one's for you! You might think it's the wrong one, but there's more to come in this series. You've dragged me to the dark side. Can't get that shoo-fly out of my head! Thank you for all the answers and help you've given me online!

To my writerly girlfriends, I am so lucky to have

your friendship, your empathy, and your wisdom. What would this job be without you?

A special thank you to Mike Downs for long walks and longer talks about plot holes, meddling women, and tragic backstories. You make my books better. Do you know that?

Ed, Mom, Dad—thank you for your constant support! Erin, Michael, and Kara, the best siblings in the world. Sissy, Kathy, Vicki, and Lisa—thank you all for all you do for my writing!

Eddie: always and ever you! And Winnie, too!